Naya Nuki

GIRL WHO RAN

Kenneth Thomasma

Grandview Publishing Company
Box 2863
Jackson, WY 83001

Fifteenth printing, January 1991

Printed in the United States of America

Library of Congress Cataloging-in-Publication Data

Thomasma, Kenneth.
Naya Nuki, Girl Who Ran / Kenneth Thomasma; Eunice Hundley, illustrator.—Grand Rapids, Mich. : Baker Book House, c1983.

131p. : ill.; 21 cm.—(Voyager series)

Summary: After being taken prisoner by an enemy tribe, a Shoshoni girl escapes and makes a thousand-mile journey through the wilderness in search of her own people.
ISBN 0-8010-8869-0.—ISBN 0-8010-8868-2 (pbk.)

1. Children's stories, American. 2. Indians of North America—Juvenile fiction. [1. Indians of North America—Fiction] I. Hundley, Eunice, ill. II. Title. III. Series: Voyager series (Grand Rapids, Mich.)
PZ7.T3696 Nay 1983 [Fic]—dc19 89-143272
AACR 2 MARC

To Frances and Arthur Scott
for their suggestions
and assistance;

the boys and girls
of Kelly Elementary School
in Kelly, Wyoming,
for being good listeners
and excellent critics; and

my wife, Bobby Jo,
for her encouragement and patience.

Contents

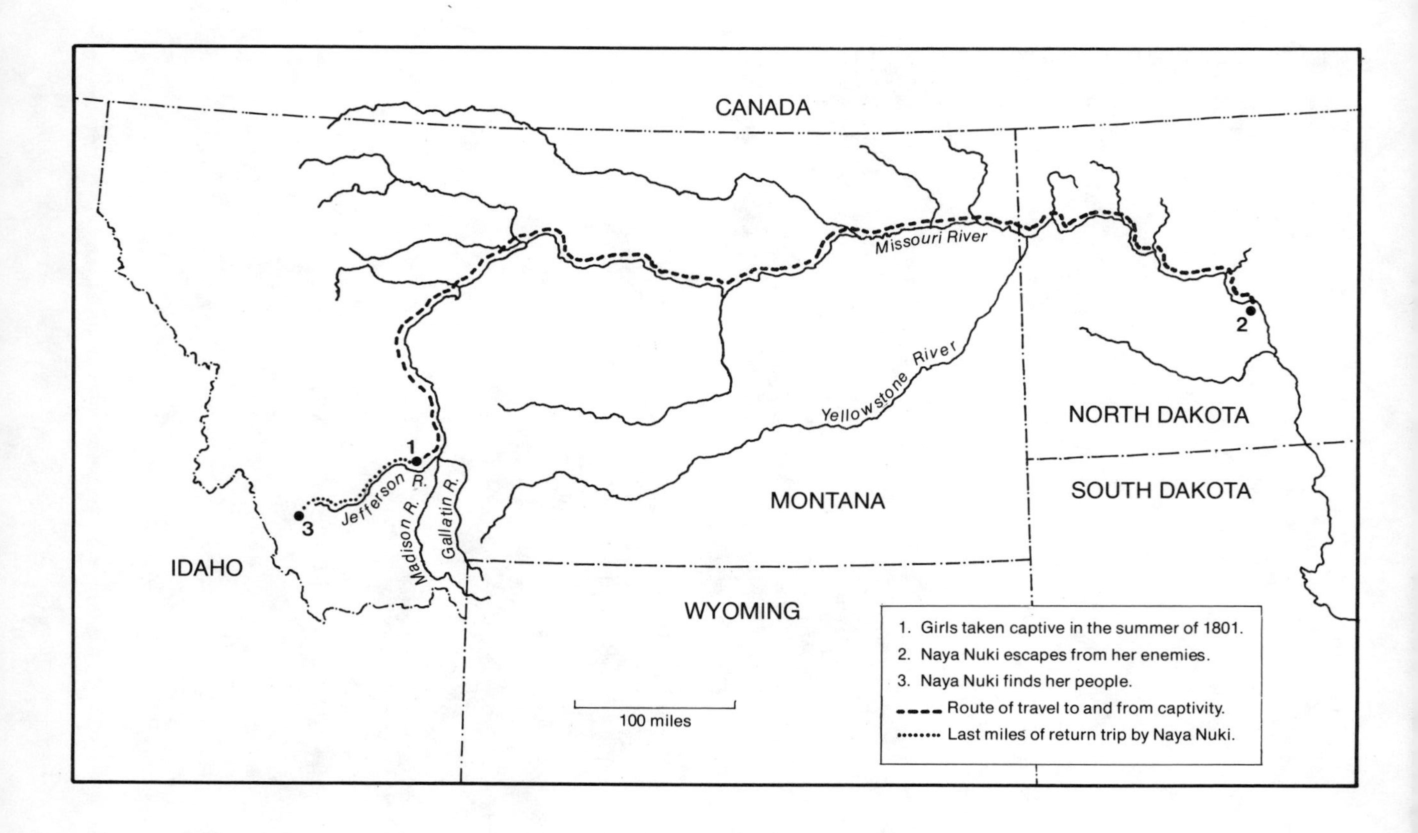
CANADA
Missouri River
Yellowstone River
NORTH DAKOTA
SOUTH DAKOTA
MONTANA
WYOMING
IDAHO
Jefferson R.
Madison R.
Gallatin R.
1
2
3
100 miles
1. Girls taken captive in the summer of 1801.
2. Naya Nuki escapes from her enemies.
3. Naya Nuki finds her people.
Route of travel to and from captivity.
Last miles of return trip by Naya Nuki.

1 On the Move

A great bald eagle circled high overhead against a clear blue sky. On a mountainside a small band of Indians moved slowly over a ridge and down into a beautiful valley. Below the soaring eagle and near the end of the slow-moving line of Indians walked two eleven-year-old Indian girls dressed in loose-fitting deerskin dresses. The girls' long black hair hung down to their waists. From the day they were born the two Shoshoni girls had been on the move, always in search of food. Many days there was not enough to eat. Many nights the girls went to sleep hungry. Even now they were hungry. They spent many hours each day gathering roots and berries, but there never seemed to be enough. Indian hunters went out every day to search for elk, deer, or other game. When they returned with meat, it was quickly eaten and usually there was little to save for the next day's meal.

Now the small band followed a faint Indian road that was no more than a wide trail. They were just coming out of the Lemhi Valley in Idaho and into western Montana. In 1801, however, there were no states of Idaho or Montana. In fact, no white man had even been in this mountain land. The Shoshoni Indians had only heard stories of the *tabbabone* (white man) whose skin was a pale color. The Indians knew only the seasons and not that the year was 1801 by the white man's counting.

These two Indian girls talked quietly as they followed their people. They were frightened. They knew that each step they took moved them closer to the prairie and closer to danger of attack by fierce tribes such as the Crow, the Blackfoot, and the Minnetares. These warlike tribes came to steal Shoshoni horses, to kill Shoshoni warriors, and to take their women and children prisoner.

The Shoshoni Indians had to go to the prairie to hunt buffalo. They needed meat for food, hides for clothing and shelter, and bones for tools. Without dried buffalo meat for the long winter, many of the tribe would starve to death. The Shoshonis must risk the chance of attack. They must have buffalo.

The Shoshonis had many fine horses but did not have rifles. The skillful hunters could ride swiftly among the stampeding buffalo and shoot arrow after arrow into a giant beast until it dropped to the earth to die. The hunt was exciting and dangerous, but one buffalo could mean hundreds of pounds of meat and a large hide for making robes and moccasins.

Sacajawea and Naya Nuki knew that horses helped their hunters to kill the wild animals. "I sometimes wish we did not have horses," whispered Naya Nuki. "Then maybe the fierce tribes from the prairie would not come to steal and kill."

"They would still come," replied Sacajawea. "They would still kill and take prisoners."

"Then I wish the buffalo would come to our home valley so we would not have to make this dangerous

journey away from our mountains. I have great fear we shall be attacked," said Naya Nuki.

It was a warm, sunny afternoon. Billowing white clouds drifted across the sky. Naya Nuki and Sacajawea were tall, thin eleven-year-old girls with lots of energy. But after a long day of walking behind the Indian men mounted on horses, both girls were tired and hungry.

Naya Nuki needed only a little time for rest and some much-needed food and a surge of energy came back to her. She was one of the strongest of the children in her village and could run further and faster than any boy or girl, even those older than she.

Naya Nuki loved to be moving, each day seeing familiar sights that she remembered from other trips over these same Indian roads. Water in the high mountain streams was clear and cold. Wildflowers filled the meadows, and the sky seemed bluer than ever.

When the men decided to stop, they picked a dry, level spot to camp. It was surrounded by willow bushes and near a fast-moving stream. It was chosen because it was well hidden from view, with plenty of firewood and good water nearby.

Right away Sacajawea and Naya Nuki began their task of helping to build shelters for the band. Trimmed sticks were used to make a frame for the small shelters. Woven mats and some animal hides were used for a covering. In less than an hour the shelters were up and would protect them from the wind and keep out the rain if it should come.

After the shelters were built, the girls and the women gathered firewood, picked berries, and dug roots. Every member of the village had work to do to make survival possible. A village had only thirty to forty members. There were just enough to protect each other and still be a small enough group to move quickly in case of danger.

This summer had been a hard one for all Indians. Big game animals were scarce. Very little rain had fallen and seeds were hard to find. Naya Nuki and Sacajawea had that familiar feeling of an empty stomach, but it was not usually this bad until late winter, when food supplies always ran low.

Naya Nuki and Sacajawea were searching for roots after their shelters were built.

"I hope we have a good hunt of the great buffalo," said Sacajawea.

"I could eat a whole buffalo liver. I'm so hungry," answered Naya Nuki.

"I'll take the heart and the tongue. We will eat these parts without cooking them. They taste good without cooking and cooking takes too long," said Sacajawea.

Hungry Indians often ate the tender parts of the buffalo raw. Leftover meat would be cut into thin strips and laid in the sun to dry. The dried meat would not spoil and could be used during the winter.

Seeds were gathered all summer and fall. They were ground to make a flour that could be formed into small cakes. Roots were dug, mashed, and dried. Snares were set to catch wildcats, coyotes, rabbits, and other small animals. Grasshoppers were used to make a soup or crushed and made into a paste that was dried in the sunshine. The largest grasshoppers were often roasted on the end of a stick that was held over the hot coals of a fire; then the grasshoppers were eaten right from the stick.

Naya Nuki and Sacajawea walked back to the camp with their woven reed baskets full of camas roots.

"My brother, Cameahwait, has been chosen to stand guard tonight for the first time. He will have to have much courage to stand alone in the dark, watching and listening for the enemy," said Sacajawea proudly.

"He is strong and brave. I will sleep well knowing Cameahwait is out there while we rest," said Naya Nuki.

Soon the smell of roasting camas roots filled the air near the campsite. Camas roots are much like potatoes, and are delicious when roasted. On this night there would be no meat, just camas roots, some seeds, and berries. In a few days fires would no longer be allowed for fear that the enemy would see the smoke and discover the tribe. All food would be eaten cold.

The children loved to sit close to a warm fire as darkness brought on the chill of the mountain night. They were always eager to listen to the stories told by the brave warriors and hunters. There were stories of great hunts when many buffalo were killed, when everyone had plenty to eat, and when even women and children had moccasins made of buffalo hide.

The children liked stories of big battles. In the old way of fighting, enemy warriors lined up facing each other and stood in one place, ducking behind rawhide shields and shooting arrows at each other from a distance. They would fight all day, with few warriors getting hurt. They never charged or got very close.

One day the Shoshoni warriors lined up to fight. The

enemy warriors, holding guns they had gotten from the white man, hid behind their shields. When these deadly fire sticks exploded, they sent iron balls into the Shoshoni braves. The helpless Shoshonis were mowed down as fast as the enemy could reload and fire. Terrified by this new magic, the survivors ran for their lives.

Other stories told of how the Shoshonis traded with the friendly Ute tribes for horses. With the horse the Shoshoni warrior and hunter could ride as swiftly as a deer. With horses the Shoshoni could ride out onto the prairie to hunt and never be caught by the enemy.

There were only a few stories around the campfire on this night. All the stories were about great buffalo hunts of the past. After the stories, a special buffalo dance was held to please the spirits of the hunt.

The main fire out in the large, open, level area was built up to a bright blaze. A brave covered with a hairy buffalo robe and wearing a real-looking buffalo headdress danced around the fire to the loud beat of the drums. Around and around he went. In and out from the fire's edge he danced, faster and faster. Up and down he threw his head, with the horns coming very close to the crowd first and then almost reaching into the fire as the dancer moved in and out and around and around.

Then came ten dancing hunters carrying spears, knives, and bows and arrows. They danced in a large circle far from the fire at first. The glow of the brightly burning fire cast flickering light and shadows on the warriors. It was a thrill for Naya Nuki and Sacajawea and all the children to see this magnificent dance. They tapped their feet and clapped their hands to the beat of the drums.

Now the buffalo dancer began dancing faster and faster as the drummers picked up the tempo. The hunters began to go faster around the large circle. As they did they began to close their circle slowly around the lone buffalo dancer. Excitement grew. Naya Nuki could feel her heart beating as the dance neared its end. In her imagination she could see a real hunt with the braves riding in for the kill.

Now the hunters closed their circle around the one in the buffalo costume. It seemed as though they would knock him into the flames. When the drummers' beat reached its fastest tempo, one of the hunters raised his spear and lunged at the buffalo dancer. He purposely missed the buffalo dancer by only inches. The buffalo dancer fell to the ground, thrashing about wildly. More lunges with spears followed. Each spear hit inches from the fallen dancer. Then the buffalo dancer lay still. The drums stopped. All was silent for a moment. The hunter making the kill uttered a shrill cry that pierced the silence of the night. Instantly the drummers resumed a slow, steady beat, and the fallen figure in the buffalo costume was carried off by the hunters. This dance was done to please the spirits and to bring good luck in the real buffalo hunt.

This dance was short. Sometimes dances would last far into the night. Tonight the campfires would be covered early and the camp kept dark for protection. From now on there would be no more fires and no more dancing until the people returned safely from the prairie.

2
The Attack

The excitement of the dance was over. Everyone moved toward the shelters. Naya Nuki could feel the chill of the night air in this high mountain valley. The Indians spoke in soft voices as they entered their shelters. Inside her shelter Naya Nuki lay down on her woven reed mat and curled up in her deerhide blanket. She lay still and thought about the buffalo dance. She was so hungry for meat. She imagined a large slice of buffalo liver just for her. The thought made her stomach feel even more empty as she changed position on her mat. Then she thought of the danger of ambush by enemy tribes. What was it like for young Cameahwait standing guard in the dark far from camp, alone, straining to see or hear the enemy, ready to shout the warning, ready to fight to protect his people? Soon a tired Naya Nuki fell into a peaceful sleep.

Each morning began in much the same way. Older women rose first as the eastern sky showed the first signs of light. Hot coals that had been carefully covered with dirt and sod the night before were uncovered. The still-hot coals were fanned and dry wood added. Soon the bright flames spread light in the predawn darkness.

When Naya Nuki was awakened by her older sister,

she felt stiff and cold. Her empty stomach made her feel weak. She crawled from her shelter as the eastern sky was aglow with the promise of warm sunlight. There was dew on the grass and the willow leaves. This morning was different. No fires were burning. No firewood needed to be gathered. The camp seemed cold and frightening. Naya Nuki missed the brightness and the warmth of the morning fires. She hoped that the hunt would end soon, and that they could return to the safety of their mountains.

Naya Nuki met Sacajawea and they hurried to the stream.

"This water is so good. It makes my empty stomach feel better," whispered Sacajawea.

Naya Nuki splashed the cold water on her face and the back of her neck.

"I feel better, too," sighed Naya Nuki. "I have two deerskins to fill with water. I'll walk back with you as soon as they're filled."

Dried berries, some raw roots, and stems from plants made up a meager breakfast. With no wood to gather and no cooking to do, it did not take long to break camp. The sun was still low in the sky when the band began moving.

To keep from being seen easily, the Shoshoni traveled away from the stream and away from the main trail. As they followed the stream at a distance, the banks widened gradually. After three days' travel without fires, they came into view of the great mountain shaped like a beaver's head. This landmark was used by all Indians who traveled in this area.

Three more days of travel brought the group close to

the "place where the waters meet," as the Indians called it. Here the Jefferson, the Madison, and the Gallatin rivers, as they are called now, join to make the mighty Missouri River.

The Shoshoni camp was made only a few hours' travel from the great river. Some fish were caught and a small deer killed. There was a little meat for everyone. Not one bit was wasted. Almost the entire deer was eaten, even soft parts of the hooves. The skin was stretched, scraped, and dried to be used for clothing, blankets, or material for shelter.

The prairie wasn't far. Soon buffalo hunting would begin. The danger of enemy attack increased. More lookouts were posted at night. Each day scouts on horseback went far ahead to look for the enemy.

The morning was cool and damp when Naya Nuki came out of her shelter. She shivered from the chill of the damp air. The sky seemed heavy with low-hanging clouds.

Naya Nuki and Sacajawea started their walk to the river through the dense willow bushes.

"Today we see the place where the waters meet. We will see the great river. It will be so exciting," whispered Naya Nuki.

"Yes, the big water will lead us to the prairie and the buffalo. Soon we will eat all the meat we want," added Sacajawea.

"Maybe I will have a buffalo robe for winter. That is the best gift I could ever want," said Naya Nuki.

Even as the girls talked, a scout was riding as fast as his pony would carry him toward the campsite. In minutes Naya Nuki and Sacajawea heard the man's shouts.

"The enemy is coming. Prepare for attack. Warriors mount up for the battle."

Naya Nuki and Sacajawea stood looking at each other for a few seconds before they turned to run. The enemy warriors were only a few miles away and were riding swift horses toward the campsite. There was great confusion for a few minutes and then the campsite was deserted. The women and children scattered and sought hiding places. The men took positions to defend their people.

Naya Nuki and Sacajawea hid in the dense willows. Naya Nuki dug under a pile of branches left in a heap during the flood season. She burrowed her way under and completely out of sight. Sacajawea lay down in the dense stalks of the willow bushes and tried to cover herself with leaves and dead branches.

Soon explosions came from the enemies' fire sticks. The guns drove off the defending Shoshoni warriors. Then the search of the willows began. Sacajawea was found first. She jumped up and tried to escape by running into the shallow river. An enemy warrior rode out into the water and grabbed her. He lifted her thin frame onto his horse and rode off.

It took much longer to find Naya Nuki. She held herself still with fear. It was hard to breathe. A dog led the enemy to Naya Nuki as she lay huddled and cramped under the pile of branches and twigs. The dog stood barking and pawing at the brush. An enemy warrior, his face covered with war paint, pulled her out by her hair and lifted her onto his horse. Naya Nuki was taken back to the campsite under guard. There were Sacajawea and several other women and children who had been taken captive.

The bows and arrows of the Shoshoni warriors could not match the guns of the raiding enemy braves. Many horses were captured. Four Shoshoni warriors lay dead. The confusion lasted only a few minutes and the battle ended.

Naya Nuki and Sacajawea stood near each other in the group of prisoners, afraid to speak. Their guards shouted orders to the frightened prisoners, telling them not to move, not to speak, and that death would come quickly if they did not obey. The attack had come so quickly that it was hard to realize what had happened.

The morning had been so peaceful and now suddenly everything had changed. The Shoshoni had been scattered. Some were dead. Some were prisoners, and some had escaped. What happened during those few minutes on this summer morning would change Naya Nuki's and Sacajawea's lives forever.

Soon all the enemy warriors returned to the campsite. Quickly the captives were separated. Each was forced to walk next to an enemy on horseback. The long line of riders began moving back toward the meeting of the waters and the great river. The riders were far enough apart so the prisoners could not speak to each other. They could only walk along wondering what would happen next. Escape was impossible. There was no chance of rescue by Shoshoni warriors. There were too many enemy warriors, and they had the deadly fire sticks. Naya Nuki, Sacajawea, and the others could only obey and go along with their captors.

In a short time the procession came to the place

where the waters meet. By noon the clouds moved east and the sky cleared. The sun soon made walking next to a horse hot and dusty. Naya Nuki counted the prisoners. There were six women and nine children. The pace was fast. Prickly pear cactus grew everywhere, and the thorns went through the deerskin moccasins, causing the captives' feet to swell and become very sore. At every rest stop, thorns were pulled out and feet soaked in water. The rest stops were short, and there was never enough time to remove all the thorns from aching feet.

The march ended late in the day. Naya Nuki was exhausted, sore, and hungry, but from the time she was first captured she began to think about escape. There was no chance now. The prisoners were too closely guarded, but that didn't stop Naya Nuki from thinking about escape.

Camp was made in the open a half a mile from the great river, but close to a clear, cool creek coming down from a high mountain valley. The prisoners were all herded into a small circle. A rider moved close to them and began speaking in the Shoshoni language. He told the women and children that they would be treated well if they obeyed. He told them they would die if they tried to escape. He said they would be guarded closely night and day. Their hands and feet would be tied at night until their captors were sure that they would not try to escape.

When he turned and rode off, guards separated the prisoners so they could not speak to each other. They were allowed to soak their swollen feet in the cool water of the swift-flowing stream and were given dried buffalo meat and roasted camas roots to eat. Naya Nuki ate the food eagerly. She knew she would need her strength when it came time to escape. She watched her guards closely, but even if a guard were not watching, the camp was in an open area, making escape impossible.

3

The Long March East

Naya Nuki wondered where she was being taken. What would happen to her when they did arrive at the end of this awful journey? Again she thought about escape. When the time was right, she would gain her freedom some way, somehow.

That night all the prisoners were tied tightly with leather thongs. Guards were on duty all night to watch the prisoners. Naya Nuki could not get to sleep. She remembered the stories told to her before her capture. Prisoners were taken far away and sold as slaves, never to return to their people. She told herself that first night that, no matter how far they took her and no matter what her captors did to stop her, some day she would escape and return to her home in the mountains.

Naya Nuki woke often that night. Her wrists and ankles ached from the tightly tied strips of hide. When the long night finally ended and morning came, the guards untied the prisoners. It was hard even to stand up at first. Her legs were numb, sore, and stiff. Soon her circulation improved. It felt good just to be able to move again.

Breakfast was more buffalo meat and camas roots. Naya Nuki drank lots of cold water with her food. Before the sun came over the eastern mountains, the march began anew. Prisoners were reminded that to try to escape would mean sure death. As before, the prisoners were kept separate. Each one had to walk next to a rider, which made it impossible to talk to the others.

Feet that were still sore from the day before again felt the jabs of the dense prickly pear. But the pace was slower and some of the cactus could be avoided.

Naya Nuki spent much of her time looking in every direction to memorize landmarks, places to hide, and the best route to follow after escaping. She knew someday she would pass this way on her trip home.

For now escape was still too dangerous. The prisoners were all watched every minute. Naya Nuki saw how their route followed the great river. Not too closely, because the river twisted and turned through the valley like a giant snake. To follow the river's edge would mean traveling great distances around each turn, one after another. Naya Nuki saw that the route that she was walking as a prisoner was sometimes more than a mile from the great river.

Day after day the routine was the same. The prisoners were up before daylight. They were forced to work while they were watched closely. They gathered wood for fires, hauled water, and baked camas roots. Breakfast was always dried buffalo meat and camas roots.

Naya Nuki felt an emptiness inside as the journey took the group out of the mountains and onto the wide-open prairie. She so wanted to escape before they were too far from the mountains. However, there was no chance. The guards were always watching the prisoners' every move and could easily track down any who tried to escape.

Soon great herds of buffalo were seen everywhere. Now there was fresh meat for every meal. Naya Nuki had never seen such great numbers of buffalo. Never before had she had so much food. Never had she seen so many precious buffalo skins. The buffalo hides made the very best and strongest moccasins. Buffalo-hide clothes and blankets were the best of all. They were warmer, more comfortable, and lasted three times as long as deer and elkhide.

Soon Naya Nuki could no longer see the mountains. The prairie seemed to be growing larger and larger. Still the desire to escape burned inside of her. She could see for miles across the vast, rolling landscape. The river was always in sight. Cottonwood trees and willows lined the banks of the great river. In some places at the river's edge steep cliffs rose above the water. High bluffs were carved out here and there.

Naya Nuki remembered one day on the long journey as one of her happiest since being captured. It was the day that all the prisoners were allowed to come together once again. They were permitted to talk to each other for the first time since becoming prisoners. They were even allowed to sleep at night without being tied up. There were still many guards watching their every move. There were daily warnings that to try to escape would mean death.

Naya Nuki and Sacajawea talked every chance they had. They were so happy to be together again. When the guards were not near enough to hear, Naya Nuki talked to Sacajawea about escape. For the first time Sacajawea talked about the impossibility of escape. She talked about how far they would have to travel to get back to the mountains. She wondered if they would ever be able to get back to their people if they could reach the mountains. Naya Nuki could see that Sacajawea might not want to try to escape at all.

Even this did not change Naya Nuki's mind. She would escape even if she had to do it alone. As she thought about it, the word *alone* rang in her mind. It filled her with fear at first. But the more she thought about escaping alone the more she got used to the idea. Then she thought that maybe other prisoners would make an escape, and she would go with them even if Sacajawea didn't. The thought of leaving her best friend Sacajawea made her heart heavy with sadness. They would probably never see each other again.

Naya Nuki continued to watch for landmarks and tried to remember each new one, along with the many others the war party had already passed. She looked for large islands in the great river, high bluffs, waterfalls, large streams that flowed into the great river, and anything that was unusual along the way.

If Naya Nuki were to make a successful escape, she would have to know the land, the best hiding places, and the safest route to follow on her long journey back to the mountains. The great river would help to lead her home, but Naya Nuki would have to know where she was and how far she had to go before reaching the mountains.

One night, in the deep darkness, Naya Nuki and Sacajawea lay whispering softly while the guard was furthest from them.

"I have been watching the land around us as we walk each day. There are many places to hide and much tall grass to conceal us as we travel home after our escape. I know we can do it together, Sacajawea. There is nothing that will stop me from escaping and going back to our mountains. When the right day comes, we shall escape. I know we can do it. We must do it, you and I," whispered Naya Nuki.

"Escape is impossible now. They watch us all the time, day and night. If we did escape, they would be sure to follow us on horses and death would come to us. Great bears, wolves, or other enemy warriors could find us before we got to the mountains. Now we have plenty of food and are safe from harm. We will talk about escape another day. Now we talk for nothing," answered Sacajawea softly.

Naya Nuki was saddened by Sacajawea's words. Naya Nuki felt lonely and abandoned. She talked to Sacajawea about other things and then lay silently looking up at the bright stars on this cold, clear night. She thought about Sacajawea's words for a long time. If Sacajawea did not want to escape, Naya Nuki would go alone. She could travel swiftly alone. She could run fast if she had to. She could hide well in time of danger. She could climb trees to escape wild animals. She could find her own food. She could do it alone. She would do it alone if no one else would go. She lay awake for hours thinking about escape. She enjoyed her thoughts and slept soundly when sleep finally did come.

After each long day's march, the captives were forced to erect shelters, go for water, gather wood, cook meals, and scrape the hides of freshly-killed buffalo. When finally their work was done, they were allowed to go to the stream to rinse the dust and the dirt from their bodies and to eat their evening meal.

Mosquitoes were thick on the prairie and their bites itched continually. The prickly pear was gone now, and Indian roads made travel easier.

Several times on the journey other Indian hunting parties were met. Indian encampments were visited and endless talks held. The prisoners knew their long march was nearly over when tribes of Indians came by who dressed like their captors and spoke the same language.

After forty-one sleeps the long trek ended at a village of long houses. Here lived several hundred Minnetare Indians. Their long houses were made of large timbers and earth. They stretched for great distances. Smoke rose from holes in the roof at regular intervals along the buildings.

Naya Nuki had never seen such places to sleep and cook. She took in all the strange sights, smells, and sounds of this huge village. Never before had she seen so many people in one place.

There was great excitement when the war party came into view. All stood looking at the prisoners and the many fine horses taken in battle. There was much shouting and loud talking as people circled around and around the weary travelers. Children pushed closer for a better look. Dogs barked and raced in and out among the crowd. Naya Nuki was frightened and wondered what would happen next in this dreadful place and among these strange people.

Soon the crowd quieted down and people began to go back to their regular activities. That night a great feast was held. After the food came a wild celebration with large fires, dancing, tales of the battle, and much rhythmic chanting by all.

Naya Nuki and the other prisoners were given food and put into a section of a long house at the very end of the building. A guard stood by the only door that led to the outside. He seemed unhappy about having to stand guard while the others celebrated.

Naya Nuki ate well and was very tired from the long march. Even with the deafening noise of the celebration nearby, she fell asleep on a skin mat on the floor of this huge long house.

When the celebration ended and all was quiet, Naya Nuki woke up. She had dreamed she was with her mother back in her own village. Naya Nuki loved her mother. She longed to see her again, to help her with her work, to be near her, and to show her the love she felt for her. Yes, Naya Nuki would plan her escape, and she would carry it out successfully. She would return to those she loved. No enemy, no wild animal, and no hardship could hold her back.

Naya Nuki remembered the time her baby brother died. She had watched her mother burn the baby's cradel, which is Shoshoni custom. She had watched as in grief her mother cut all her own hair off and took a sharp stone and gashed her legs until the blood flowed freely from many wounds. Naya Nuki saw the great love of a mother for her child. Naya Nuki loved her mother more than anyone else in the world. No, nothing would stop Naya Nuki from escaping. She would return home or die trying.

4

Slavery

At the first light in the eastern sky the prisoners were aroused. Enemy women came and each one motioned for a prisoner to follow her. This way all the prisoners were separated. Naya Nuki and Sacajawea would see very little of each other from this time on.

Naya Nuki was taken to a long house at the far end of the village. She was forced to work for an old woman from before dawn till after dark. The woman beat her for no reason at all. Naya Nuki worked hard gathering wood, carrying water, digging roots, picking berries, grinding grain, scraping animal skins, and making mud to repair holes in the long houses.

Naya Nuki worked as hard as she could. She never caused the old woman any trouble. She did even more than was expected of her. After a while the old woman stopped beating her. Naya Nuki was a model prisoner. Other women wanted her to work for them. They all thought Naya Nuki was the best of the prisoners. None dreamed that Naya Nuki was daily thinking and planning for her escape.

While gathering wood on a high hill above the village, Naya Nuki carefully studied the winding of the great river. She looked for the best way of escape, the best way to run on her dash to freedom. Her heart pounded as she thought of that moment of escape.

Naya Nuki waited for chances to steal some badly-needed things for her escape and long journey home. She needed a sharp object to use as a knife and a buffalo skin for warmth. She would make extra pairs of moccasins in secret. She would hide a supply of dried meat and berries, and some strips of hide. Naya Nuki had to be careful not to be discovered stealing or hiding food. If she were caught, she could suffer a slow, painful end to her life.

Naya Nuki continued to work very hard for the old woman, who was the mother of one of the enemy chiefs. Naya Nuki was always the first one to get up in the morning. She would brush mounds of dirt from the hot coals of yesterday's fire. Dry wood was added and the fire fanned into flame. Next Naya Nuki was off to fetch more wood and get water.

Soon the old woman would rise and come out of the long house to warm herself by the fire. Naya Nuki would already be coming back with her arms full of wood or with skins filled with fresh water. Naya Nuki always acted as if she were happy with her new life. Her hard work and good behavior meant she was trusted more and more and watched less.

One morning, as the sun was high, Naya Nuki worked very hard scraping many hides, which would soon be stretched on racks to dry in the hot sun. Most of the hides were buffalo, the best and most valuable. To steal one would be dangerous, but Naya Nuki wanted one so much. It was a necessary part of her escape plan. She must have one. She would steal it soon.

Naya Nuki planned to rise a little earlier than usual. In the morning darkness she would pass by the stack of hides, quickly grab one and carry it to the tree-covered hill, and hide it in a pile of brush. She would be back before she was missed. Her heart once again pounded as she thought of this dangerous plan. Naya Nuki scraped harder and faster now to hide the trembling caused by her excitement. The next morning a hide would be hers.

That night Naya Nuki rolled and tossed, finding it hard to get to sleep because of her excitement. She woke up often during the night. She was up early as planned. The sky was cloudy. There was no moonlight, and the wind would muffle any sound she might make.

Quickly Naya Nuki passed the pile of skins, taking one and hurrying up the familiar path in the darkness. She hid the skin and returned quickly to uncover the fire and go about her work as usual.

Naya Nuki tried not to look at the old woman. She thought the old woman would need only to look into her eyes and see the guilt that must be in them. She did her best to act as though nothing unusual had happened; and the old woman paid little attention to Naya Nuki on this day.

The wind was cold, and Naya Nuki was ordered to build the fire higher to warm the old woman better. She obeyed willingly to avoid looking the woman in the eyes.

With the buffalo hide safely hidden, Naya Nuki would turn her attention to getting a knife. Little did she know that this same day held a welcome surprise for her.

By afternoon the sky had cleared, and the sun was shining brightly. Naya Nuki was on a trip for water. At the creek that ran to the great river, she stopped at a favorite bathing spot where the water was deep and still. She plunged in to wash the dust and the dirt from her dry skin. When she came back to the surface her toe stung with a sharp pain. She raised her foot above the water's surface as she floated on her back. Blood streamed from her toe. Whatever she had hit on the bottom was so sharp that it had cut through the skin.

On the bank, Naya Nuki held her toe tightly to stop the flow of blood. Many minutes passed before she could stem the flow. When it did stop, Naya Nuki entered the water very carefully. With her eyes open, she slowly swam headfirst for the bottom. There on the bottom lay a shiny metal object. Carefully she picked it up and returned to the surface. In her hand she held a knife with a bone handle and a metal blade. She paid no attention to her toe, which was bleeding again. With her newfound treasure, she ran immediately to the nearby willow bushes and quickly buried the precious knife. She marked the spot with a large rock and rushed back to the creek.

Once again she stopped the flow of blood from the cut on her toe. She carefully covered the signs of blood on the rocky bank, filled her water skins, and returned to her work.

Who lost the knife? Surely the owner would return to look for it. Did I hide it well enough? Will it be found? Should I hide it in a better place? All these questions raced through Naya Nuki's mind, but she stayed away from that spot on the creek for several days. When she did return she saw from a short distance that the rock marking the knife's hiding place was still right where she had put it.

In one day Naya Nuki had gotten a buffalo skin and a knife, the two things she needed most for her escape and survival. She wanted to escape before someone discovered her hidden treasures. Her mind was filled with plans, with fears, and with hope, all at the same time.

Naya Nuki could hardly think straight and sometimes did not hear the old woman give orders. Several times she scolded Naya Nuki for not paying attention. Naya Nuki had to force herself to listen, to remember, and to work. She must not let up. She must not let the old one know that she was planning something.

Naya Nuki made extra moccasins and hid them. She gathered up a secret supply of dried meat and berries. She was ready for the most important day of her life, the day of her escape.

The time for escape must be perfect, a dark night with a rainstorm to cover her tracks. Without rain, enemy warriors could easily track her down. Naya Nuki would run when the time was right, not before. She must not fail.

From now on her eyes searched the sky each afternoon for an approaching storm. She had memorized the habits of every member of the village. Naya Nuki knew every trail from the village and the location of every building and corral. She studied the stars, which on clear nights would guide her when the great river could not be seen. Naya Nuki's every spare minute was filled with thinking, planning, and preparing for escape.

Four days after getting the knife and the buffalo skin,

Naya Nuki had a rare meeting with Sacajawea. What Sacajawea told Naya Nuki frightened her greatly.

"I have been sold to a *tabbabone,*" Sacajawea told Naya Nuki. "I will do his work, eat his food, and he will give me beads and wonderful things the white man has. He will take me to the big village of the white man called Saint Louis. Naya Nuki, I am so excited but also sad. I hope I shall see you again. Maybe a *tabbabone* will buy you, too."

"Sacajawea, you are my good friend. I too hope we will meet again some day." Naya Nuki said no more. Sacajawea had to leave. She turned to leave but stopped once to look back at Naya Nuki before going around a long house and out of sight, maybe forever.

Naya Nuki was more afraid and nervous than ever. What if she were sold? What if she were taken even further away from her home? What about her knife and buffalo skin, hidden and ready to go? She must leave soon, but when would the rain come at night? Several storms came and went during the afternoon hours, but they did not last. Would her chance come in time?

5 *A Night to Run*

It was an October afternoon and the evening meal was ready. The heat of the day was still present. It was warm and muggy. The air was still. Suddenly the wind came up, raising the dust. The temperature began to fall. The western sky grew dark as the sun was going down. A storm was building.

Naya Nuki's heart began to race. This could be the night. She was hardly able to chew her food. Thunder and lightning filled the air. At sunset the rain started. The women rushed to bury the red-hot coals of their fires. Everyone took shelter in the long houses. Fires were built under each hole in the roofs of the long houses, but the wind caused the smoke to remain inside the houses. It became so bad that the fires had to be put out. Everyone huddled in buffalo skins to keep warm. Many went to sleep early.

Naya Nuki crouched in her corner. She listened to every sound around her. Her heart beat so fast and so hard that she was afraid others could hear it pound inside her body.

Outside the wind howled, and the thunder was deafening. Bright flashes of lightning lit up the long house for a few seconds at a time. The Great Spirit surely must be angry. The heavens seemed to roar.

Naya Nuki remembered other storms when she and her brothers and sisters huddled close to their mother until the storm had passed. Now Naya Nuki would use the weather she once had feared to help her in a desperate run to freedom.

The wind and rain continued. The thunder and lightning came and went. The long house grew quiet. It was very dark inside as Naya Nuki waited. Time passed slowly.

With the fires out, Naya Nuki could move unseen. Even if her movement were noticed, she could not be recognized. Now was the perfect time. The hours of waiting in the darkness were over. It was time to leave. Time for escape.

Naya Nuki moved slowly toward the door, being careful not to disturb the sleeping forms. She had memorized where each person slept, and made her way easily through the darkness toward the opening.

Once outside the long house, Naya Nuki walked slowly in the direction of the tree-covered hill and the pile of brush where the buffalo hide was hidden. She had moved the knife to this same hiding place before dawn just two days earlier. Also hidden there were some dried food and three pairs of moccasins.

As Naya Nuki left the village in the pouring rain, she began to run. Distant lightning gave her just enough light to make out familiar surroundings. Soon she reached the pile of brush and quickly uncovered the precious items so necessary for her survival.

Naya Nuki quickly tied everything securely inside the buffalo skin. She tied the knife to her side, took a deep breath, and began to run. She headed north and west

away from the village. She had looked at the route many times from the hill near the village, but now it was dark and the rain and the wind seemed to change everything. No stars were visible to guide her.

Naya Nuki ran as fast as she could without slipping and falling. An accident now could ruin everything. Naya Nuki was alone. There would be no one to help her. She could not afford to make a mistake. To fail now would mean certain death. She must move as fast as possible and as far as possible.

As Naya Nuki ran, she was so busy paying attention to her efforts that she forgot her fears. All her senses were needed to help her stay on her feet and keep running. She ran for hours before she even thought of how tired she was getting.

It was more than five hours before Naya Nuki stopped running for the first time to catch her breath and to rest for a few minutes. The rain continued, but far ahead Naya Nuki could see a star. The storm was ending. She had hoped for more rain. By morning a search party would mount horses and come looking for her. If they found her trail, she wouldn't have a chance. It must rain some more.

Naya Nuki cut her rest short and was once again running through the darkness. She had fallen several times but rolled over and over and was not hurt.

Soon the stars were again covered by clouds as another squall line moved in. Lightning and thunder once again filled the night. The welcome rain beat down on Naya Nuki's face, giving her new energy. She forgot her tired, aching muscles and ran on and on into the stormy night.

Naya Nuki's next stop was at dawn. The eastern sky behind her was brightening. During the long night she had crossed several small streams. Now she had come to a large river flowing south toward the great river. It was swift, wide, and deep.

Naya Nuki had learned her wilderness travel lessons well. Study the current, look for an eddy on the opposite shore for a safe landing spot, go upstream, walk out into the current as far as possible, then begin to swim and float downstream and across the current to a safe landing on the opposite side.

Naya Nuki went upstream and picked her route carefully. She eased her tired legs into the cold water and began her crossing. She had room to spare and easily floated into the quiet eddy of deep water. Reaching the far bank, she scrambled up to level ground. She had crossed her first large river safely. Naya Nuki felt proud of herself. She moved on.

As daylight came, heavy dark clouds filled the sky. The air was cool. From a small hill a tired Naya Nuki looked in every direction. In the distance to the south, over the rolling prairie, she could faintly see a line of trees and now and then a bluff cut by the great river. The line of trees looked like a giant snake as it followed the twisting riverbed. The sight made Naya Nuki feel very good. The river would be her guide, her only map to show the way home. She would not let it out of her sight.

As the day brightened, the rain stopped. Now she must find a place to hide. She must not be seen. Daylight was her enemy, ready to betray her. Naya Nuki was exhausted. Every muscle ached as never before.

Her feet burned with pain, but she was free, on her own, on her way home.

Naya Nuki used an old trick about hiding that she had learned from her people. Where there are no rocks, caves, willows, or trees, and just open grasslands, one digs one's hiding place. Digging carefully, without disturbing the area around her too much, Naya Nuki made a shallow trench to lie in. After covering herself with soil, Naya Nuki used a pile of grass at her side to scatter over the fresh soil. To find her, the enemy would have to walk on her.

Naya Nuki's hiding place was dug on a gentle slope far from any normal routes of travel. The damp earth felt warm around her tired body. Her belongings, wrapped in her buffalo hide, lay next to her. As weary as she was, sleep still would not come. Naya Nuki's ears were alert for sounds of anything or anyone approaching her. The grass around her was too high for her to see anything without standing up. All Naya Nuki could think of was her freedom, her escape.

When sleep did come, it was a restless sleep, filled with dreams of being chased and not being able to run. Naya Nuki woke up often and found herself shaking with fear. She did not get up until it was nearly dark. Her body ached everywhere. She was so stiff and sore that she could hardly stand. First she struggled to get to her hands and knees. She raised up on her knees and peered over the top of the grass. She could see for a great distance. There wasn't a living thing in sight.

Slowly Naya Nuki rose on wobbly legs. She stretched while looking in every direction. She reached down, picked up her bundle, and once more began moving west. As darkness closed about her, it became impossible to see the great river. In the clear sky the friendly stars would be her guide.

Naya Nuki planned to travel at night for at least five sleeps. Darkness would hide her from the enemy. Fear of capture followed her every step. She would run as much as possible during her night travel.

She had to be on guard for the great white bear (the grizzly) that prowled about at night. The bear was called by this name because the silver tips on its fur coat make it look gray and even white from a distance. This ferocious bear would attack almost without reason. Naya Nuki would not have a chance against the great white bear with its long sharp claws, with the strength of many warriors, and with speed to outrun any brave.

Wolf packs roamed the prairie in search of the weak, the lame, and the old. Naya Nuki would have to be alert every minute. She could rely only upon herself. One moment of carelessness could mean instant death.

The stiffness slowly left Naya Nuki's muscles as she moved faster and faster. Soon she began her rhythmic running in the darkness, careful not to twist her ankle or step into a hole. The sky was clear and soon the moon brightened the land enough that Naya Nuki could see her shadow.

All night Naya Nuki ran at a steady pace, with short periods of walking that served as rest periods. At every stream she drank small amounts of water. She ate no food and would go without food as long as possible. As a Shoshoni Indian, she was used to having only three or four meals a week when times were hard. Now Naya Nuki would call on all her past experiences to help her survive her long and difficult journey back to her people and the life she loved.

As the second night neared its end, Naya Nuki felt quite sure that she had not been followed. She had a great feeling of relief that she had come so far without unforeseen trouble. Somehow she would find her people. She was sure of it now. Nothing would stop her.

When dawn of the second day arrived, Naya Nuki came upon a large river much like the one she had crossed the first night. She decided to stay back about a mile from this river and find a place to hide for the day. She walked along a drainage ravine that came down from the sloping plain to this river. A large logjam had formed across the ravine during the spring runoff of melting snows. Naya Nuki climbed into this mass of jumbled logs. At the center of the huge pile she found a space large enough for her to stretch out. She leveled off this place with pieces of bark and twigs. She spread out her buffalo hide and curled up for some sleep.

Naya Nuki slept only slightly better than she had the day before. Every sound brought her wide awake and alert. A porcupine scratching on a nearby log, a coyote's piercing howl, and a raven's squawking all kept her on edge and robbed her of precious sleep.

6
Danger at Night

The sun was setting, and Naya Nuki prepared to start her third night of travel. Hunger pangs reminded her that she hadn't eaten for two nights and two days. A fast pace of travel burned up lots of energy. Her body cried out for food. Still Naya Nuki would wait until morning before eating.

Again the night was clear and the moon shone brightly. Naya Nuki had traveled only a short distance this third night when she stopped to listen and to smell. She was sure she smelled smoke. The wind was blowing lightly from the southwest. The smoke was coming from her left and its source was not far away.

Carefully Naya Nuki moved forward in the darkness. She made her way up a gentle slope through tall grass. The smoke grew thicker. Naya Nuki strained to see ahead of her. Slowly and silently she moved forward. Soon she saw the first campfire and then another and another.

Slightly below her and to her left, about a quarter of a mile away, lay an encampment of at least one hundred enemy Indians. Naya Nuki's heart pounded. What if the wind hadn't carried the smoke to her? She might have gotten too close to the camp and been discovered.

Slowly Naya Nuki backed away. She made a wide

circle north, going at least one full mile out of her way to avoid this camp. She crossed a clear, cold stream, the same one the encampment used for water. Her pace quickened as she put distance between herself and the camp. She had avoided her first dangerous obstacle.

This third night was very cold. Naya Nuki welcomed the freezing temperatures. The cold would kill the troublesome mosquitoes that had plagued her the first two nights.

Dawn came, and once again Naya Nuki stopped for a day of rest and sleep. She found a small clump of spruce trees that gave her a good hiding place among the low-hanging branches. She spread her buffalo hide on the ground under the branches and hungrily took some dried buffalo meat and a few roots from her food supply. Food never tasted better. She chewed the food slowly and finished her meal with some dried berries. After a drink of cool, sweet water, Naya Nuki lay down to sleep.

The warm sun helped her drop off to sleep. She slept better than before, waking up only three times all day. Once she woke up to see a large snake crawl over her legs. She recognized it as harmless and just watched it slither off into the tall grass.

As darkness came once again, Naya Nuki began her fourth night of travel. She walked slowly at first and ate some dried roots and berries. She drank water at every stream she crossed. The night was cold and a biting wind chilled her. She quickened her pace as her eyes adjusted to the darkness. The moon came up later each night and became smaller in size.

Naya Nuki stayed alert, listening for any unusual

sound. She used her nose to search the air for odors. She strained her eyes to see any danger. It was on this fourth night that Naya Nuki really felt alone. She kept telling herself that her only chance to make it home to her people was to stay alert and use all her skills to survive. If only Sacajawea could have come with her. Two would have a better chance of surviving. I must not waste time wishing for what can never be, she thought. I must think only of survival. Each step I take will bring me closer to home. I must think only of staying free and moving toward the mountains.

Naya Nuki's planned route home would cover about one thousand miles. In terms of present-day geography, she would have to cross nearly half of North Dakota and almost all of Montana. She would have to follow the Missouri River to its source in southwestern Montana. Naya Nuki was only eleven years old. She would need the utmost courage and skill to have even a slight chance of living through such a wilderness journey.

During the night the wind increased, and the temperature dropped. Soon the moon was covered by heavy, dark clouds. A freezing rain began to fall. Naya Nuki lowered her head and continued moving. Rain and snow mixed was followed by heavy, wet snow. It caked in Naya Nuki's hair. She wiped it out of her eyes often. It was hard to see or hear, but she continued.

Naya Nuki remembered the warmth of her people's lodges. She thought about those times when they would gather in the lodge of an aged warrior and listen to stories of brave deeds of the past. She remembered every story ever told to her.

Suddenly Naya Nuki felt great fear come over her.

She could not see anything, or hear or smell anything different. Something else told her that great danger was near.

As she stopped to wonder what could be wrong, she remembered the story of the braves who became lost in a great snowstorm. They could not see, hear, or smell. They were moving on helplessly when an old warrior cried out for all to stop. The younger braves obeyed the old one. He told them to take cover without moving any further and to wait until the storm passed. When the storm ended and the braves could look around, they found themselves on the edge of a high cliff, three hundred feet above the rocks. Only a few more steps and some or all would have fallen to their deaths. The old man had saved their lives.

Naya Nuki remained in the spot where she stood, realizing the danger of continuing. She dug a shallow trench, rolled herself in the buffalo hide, and let the heavy snow cover her. A foot of snow fell before the wind finally let up and the snow stopped falling. Naya Nuki stayed in her snow-covered cocoon. Dawn was only an hour away.

When daylight came, Naya Nuki crawled out of her warm bed and stood to look around. It was then that she trembled at the sight before her. Only a few feet away the land dropped sharply to the great river below. Naya Nuki had stopped on the edge of a two-hundred-foot bluff carved by erosion. As Naya Nuki had walked during the storm, she had gone far out of her way. Instead of walking west, she was going due south and had stopped just a few feet short of certain death.

Naya Nuki thanked the Great Spirit for being with

her and causing her to stop in time. Never again would she travel during a storm or when she could not see or hear well. Her great desire to get home must not cause her to take unnecessary chances. She must think clearly. Every decision was hers alone. Any mistake could be her last. Naya Nuki shook and shivered as she looked down at the river below.

Slowly Naya Nuki turned and walked through the deep snow. Travel was still dangerous. Not only was it daylight, but also her tracks in the snow were like a giant finger pointing right at her.

Naya Nuki took only a few steps before stopping. She would have to stay in this spot until the snow melted. She could not leave a trail that could lead to her capture. Her only choice was to stay, to wait, and to watch.

Time passed slowly. The sun was warm and bright on the white snow. The warmth felt good on Naya Nuki's tired body. She became drowsy and fought to stay awake. She rubbed snow on her face many times to keep from falling asleep.

By noon enough snow had melted for Naya Nuki to make her way safely to a distant clump of trees and bushes to hide herself from sight. She was soon lying in her buffalo skin and sleeping soundly.

The howls of coyotes woke Naya Nuki. Darkness had come to the prairie. She sat up and began preparing to leave. She took time to eat some dried roots and berries from her meager supply. Having eaten only three small meals, Naya Nuki would begin the fifth night of her long trip. She paid little attention to her hunger. Every night of safe travel took her further from the enemy and closer to home.

During this night of travel Naya Nuki crossed two wide rivers coming from the north. The water in the rivers was low now in the fall of the year compared with the high run-off times in the spring, but danger was still there. She always searched for a safe crossing. Darkness made seeing difficult. Naya Nuki was always nervous as she entered the water. Often she used a log to help her float through the deepest part of the current. River crossings used up a lot of time. She was always greatly relieved when she arrived safely on the opposite shore. The cold water refreshed her and gave her new energy. She was glad to be on solid ground and heading west.

As this fifth night of travel ended, Naya Nuki sat in some willow bushes near a small creek. The eastern sky showed a tint of light, signaling the arrival of another day. Back home this always had been Naya Nuki's favorite time of day. The early morning hours were always full of activity. Birds sang the songs of a new day. The air was clear and fresh. Cheerful morning fires were fanned into flame. Women and girls gathered wood and went for water. The morning meal was prepared and always tasted so good. In times of plenty, breakfast was the biggest meal of the day.

Gathering berries and roots was the work of the day for women and children. Men were off early to hunt and fish. Berries, roots, fish, and wild game were dried and saved for the long winter. Hides were scraped and dried.

7 *Always Alert*

Naya Nuki sat thinking of those mornings at home. The birds sang. The air was still. The water in the creek rippled over its rocky bed. She felt safer than she had since her escape and was enjoying the sights and the sounds of the early morning, but she wished she were home.

Naya Nuki's peaceful moments were broken by a rumbling noise in the distance. She recognized the sound. Quickly she left the willows and ran to a nearby cottonwood tree. She scrambled up the tree, taking her belongings with her. The sound was much louder now and a huge dust cloud could be seen in the rays of the morning sun. The rumble sounded like distant thunder.

Naya Nuki looked north and soon could see a great herd of buffalo moving directly toward the tree in which she was safely perched. The great beasts were moving at a slow trot on both sides of the creek.

The ground shook and the tree swayed as this herd of more than one thousand bison rumbled along. Naya Nuki had never seen such a sight. In minutes her tree was surrounded by these enormous animals. Dust caused Naya Nuki to sneeze often. The great bodies, heads down, seemed to roll by in an endless stream. The buffalo had huge grayish-black humps, shaggy heads, and swishing tails, and ran side by side, often bumping each other.

Naya Nuki held tightly to the shaking tree. As she looked down at this amazing sight, she could not help but think of the food and the hides that were passing just below her. She remembered that at the time of her capture her people were on their way to hunt these great beasts. Now she sat just above hundreds of them.

Naya Nuki remembered the kills the men made in a hunt the year before her capture. Her people were so hungry for meat that they ate raw the first animal killed. The favorite parts were the heart and liver. The brains, the tongue, and the most tender parts of the muscle tissue were eaten next. Never did the meat taste better.

After more buffalo were killed, meat was stripped from the bones in long, thin strands to be hung and dried. Hides were scraped and stretched to dry. The horns were saved and used for drinking vessels. Everyone worked quickly so the return to the safety of the mountains could be made as soon as possible.

How strange everything seemed now. Naya Nuki was so far from her people and all alone in a tree above a huge herd of these tremendous beasts. As most of the herd passed, Naya Nuki looked across the stream from her tree. She saw several buffalo cows and their calves straggling behind the main herd. One calf lagged far back from its mother and the herd. It was curious about everything and in no hurry.

Suddenly a pack of wolves came racing out of the trees and down the gentle slope toward the lone calf. The little one didn't have a chance. The wolves made the kill quickly, tearing open the neck of the calf. Cow

buffalo do not defend their calves when the herd is moving. The calves must keep up or run the risk of attack and death.

Naya Nuki watched as the pack of hungry wolves tore the carcass to shreds. The whole incident lasted less than an hour. After the wolves left, ravens, hawks, and other scavengers would clean any remaining meat off the bones.

When the wolves were safely out of the way, Naya Nuki climbed down from the gnarled cottonwood tree, jumped the creek, and ran west. Her first day of travel started with great excitement. She had traveled all the night before and planned to keep going all day as well. It would be exhausting, but she was much too excited to sleep.

It seemed good to be moving during the daytime. She could see much better, but so could the enemy. Naya Nuki stayed in the high grass, bushes, and trees whenever possible. She avoided any trails, roads, or places where she could be seen easily. She stopped often, looking carefully in every direction. Even when she was moving, Naya Nuki kept looking ahead and from side to side for any danger. To the south she could see the path of the great river as it meandered through the rolling plains. She could seldom see the water in the great river, only the trees and the bushes that lined its sides.

After traveling for a whole night and a whole day without sleep, Naya Nuki was very tired. She was also very hungry. She found an outcropping of rock in which grew many dwarf cedar trees. It was a perfect place to hide for the night.

Naya Nuki took time to enjoy her biggest meal since

her escape. She ate meat, roots, and berries. She had water from a nearby spring that bubbled from the earth.

She took extra time to pull grass to lay over the ground beneath the dwarf cedar trees. She made a comfortable bed, rolled up in her buffalo hide, and soon was sound asleep.

In the middle of the night, Naya Nuki woke up shivering and cold. She had rolled out of her buffalo hide. She quickly looked around and then rolled herself back in the hide and, when she was warm again, went back to sleep.

The squawk of a raven woke Naya Nuki. She sat up in the bitter cold. Dense fog was everywhere and it was hard to see even one hundred feet in any direction. Naya Nuki knew better than to move from her camp when it was impossible to see approaching danger. The sun was up for several hours before the fog lifted enough for her to travel safely.

At noon Naya Nuki came to a large river. The search for a safe crossing began. It was so much easier in the daylight. She walked north upstream along the riverbank. At several places she walked on the rocks right at the river's edge and once came to a pile of driftwood wedged between two huge rocks. Naya Nuki stopped to examine the pile of wood more closely. Soon she was digging into the pile of twigs and small branches. She smiled as she came to a cache of wild artichokes deep in the pile. These white roots, one to three inches long, are delicious and nourishing. Naya Nuki and Sacajawea often had found them in piles of driftwood. Mice collect the artichokes and store them there. Naya Nuki ate a few and put the rest with her food supply.

This river was wide but not very deep. Naya Nuki didn't bother to use a log to support her. She made sure no one was in view and entered the water to begin the crossing. She waded more than halfway across and floated slowly through a deep spot. Minutes later she waded the rest of the distance to the safety of the willow bushes on the opposite bank. She had made the crossing quickly.

Naya Nuki was shocked to see two log rafts pulled up on the bank and hidden in the willows. Indians used rafts to cross rivers and to transport buffalo meat, hides, and other goods downstream.

Immediately Naya Nuki realized the danger. Enemies could be close by. She must be careful not to walk into their view. Quickly she moved north and found a thick clump of willows. She burrowed into the center of the bushes, where she was completely out of sight. Here she waited quietly, listening for any sound of danger.

After thirty minutes in hiding, Naya Nuki formed a plan. She would move quickly from one clump of bushes to another, staying out of sight until she felt it was safe to dash to the next hiding place. It took her a long time to cover only one-half mile this way, but she would take no chances on being caught.

A half a mile from the rafts a tiny creek trickled through a ravine on its way down to the river at an angle from the northwest. Naya Nuki moved quickly into the ravine and headed away from the dangerous river, out of the view of any passers-by.

In the ravine Naya Nuki could not see very far in any direction. The ravine was twenty to thirty feet deep. She took time to climb the side of the ravine for a view of the surrounding country. She did this several times. Each time she saw nothing to cause her to change her course.

After going a mile in the ravine, Naya Nuki emerged and ran carefully through the tall grass. It seemed good to be able to see for a long distance in every direction again. She slowed her pace and was soon walking at her steady rate.

She stopped just before dark each day, always in a safe place to spend the night. She ate each night before going to sleep and each morning after getting up. She did not eat during the day but drank lots of water along the way. Even at this rate her food supply would be gone in a few days.

For two days Naya Nuki moved without trouble. On the ninth day, Naya Nuki stood on a high hill looking south toward the great river. Here she saw a huge river flowing from the south into the great river. She remembered this place well. She and her captors had camped near the meeting place of these two large rivers on the way east.

The water in the river from the south was green and clearer than the muddy brown water of the great river. Naya Nuki heard her captors talk about this river from the south. They said it came from a land where the stone was yellow. We know that Naya Nuki was looking at the Yellowstone River entering the Missouri. The place where she stood is near the present-day border between North Dakota and Montana. She looked down at this scene for a few minutes and then turned to resume her journey west.

It was late afternoon of the same day when Naya

Nuki saw dust rise in the distance directly in front of her. She rushed to a hiding place in some chokecherry bushes and watched as the dust moved closer to her. This time the dust wasn't caused by the movement of buffalo. Naya Nuki could see riders on horseback. She did not move a muscle. She counted eleven braves. They led pack horses carrying quarters of buffalo carcasses. Their hunt had been very successful. They looked tired and concentrated on the trail back to their village. They passed two hundred yards from Naya Nuki's hiding place.

Naya Nuki watched as the riders disappeared. Then she moved away from her hiding place. She stopped early that evening to pick berries and to pull some wild carrots from a damp meadow. She found a large hollow log that had been burned out by a fire. She could crawl inside with room to spare, a perfect place to spend the night.

Naya Nuki ate fresh berries and wild carrots with her dried meat and roots. She slept soundly inside the charred log and woke up only three times during the night. Usually she woke up six or eight times to look and to listen for anything that could prove dangerous.

The morning of the tenth day was clear and cold. There was frost everywhere. Naya Nuki was up before the sun touched the earth around her. Fresh berries and wild carrots tasted so good. She drank ice-cold water and began to walk west in the early morning light.

The sun warmed the earth, and Naya Nuki moved easily over the prairie. This would be a good day. She could see for miles. There were more trees now, most of which grew in ravines and near the many streams that had to be crossed. She moved at her usual steady pace.

It was midmorning when Naya Nuki saw another creek ahead of her. She sensed that there was something different about this stream. She slowed her pace and stayed low and out of sight as she came up to this creek. Here she climbed a cottonwood tree for a better view. Her caution was well taken. Just a short distance downstream and on the opposite shore were the remains of a fresh Indian camp. A large band had stayed on this site.

Naya Nuki avoided the spot by going a full mile north before crossing the creek. She moved slowly, keeping out of sight by bending low as she walked in the waist-high grass. Several times she slowly straightened up for a quick look around and then moved on.

8 *Burial Platform*

Naya Nuki was soon a safe distance from the campsite and could walk upright again. About four miles from the Indian campsite, Naya Nuki stopped suddenly. She strained her eyes to make out something straight ahead of her. A short distance more and she recognized a scene that sent chills through her whole body. As she got closer, she moved more slowly. Yes, it was a burial platform built about seven feet high on four sturdy poles. This was a common form of burial among prairie Indians.

Normally Naya Nuki would never go near such a place, but for some reason she was strangely attracted to this solemn spot. It was a place that almost no Indian would go near after the burial ceremony was finished. The spirits would not be kind to anyone who disturbed the dead. For this reason Naya Nuki felt quite safe from enemies. There would be no one else anywhere near this place.

Naya Nuki was close enough to see the sled on top of the platform, but there was no body on it. Usually the body, lying face up, was brought to the site on a sled. Then the sled was lifted up on the four poles and secured there with the body facing the sky. Naya Nuki glanced down and saw a small body in the grass beneath the platform. She could not move. She just looked at the dead child. It was a boy, about five or six years old. Many thoughts raced through her mind. She remembered deaths in her own village. She remembered again the death of her tiny brother. Death terrified Naya Nuki. At this moment she wanted to be home more than ever.

The small body of the boy was wrapped in a beautiful buffalo hide. The strong prairie winds must have blown the body from the platform. A short distance away Naya Nuki saw the body of a dog, still in its harness. Naya Nuki knew the custom. The dog belonged to the dead boy and was used to pull the sled and his master's body to the burial site. The dog was killed at the burial site and left near his master. The dog's reward was to join his master in death so that both could go to the land of the Great Spirit together.

Naya Nuki also saw a buffalo-skin bag that had fallen, spilling its contents on the ground. Near the bag lay two pairs of buffalo-hide moccasins, a necklace of beaver claws, some dried meat and roots, two bone scrapers used for cleaning animals hides, and a supply of Indian paints of various colors. These were sent with the dead boy so he could use them on his trip to the land of the Great Spirit.

Naya Nuki longed to pick up the buffalo-skin sack and fill it with the things lying on the ground. She could use most of them. She even thought about the buffalo hide wrapped around the body. These things could be had by just picking them up. She could use them to help her on her desperate struggle to get back to her own people. Naya Nuki stood without moving, silently looking at this whole scene. She knew all the taboos, the

things that one never did. No one ever touched anything that belonged to the dead. To do so would cause the evil spirits to visit the guilty one. Death could soon follow. Because that evil person had broken the taboos, the land of the Great Spirit would be closed to him after his death.

Naya Nuki backed away, touching nothing. She circled north and walked on her lonely way. All that day she thought of her childhood. It was hard to concentrate on the dangers of her own journey. Naya Nuki remembered the good times when there was plenty of food and many skins for clothing and shelters. There was even time for doing beadwork and fancy sewing. Girls made dolls and played with them for hours. Naya Nuki was especially good at sewing, using thin strands of hide pulled through the hides with needles made of fine, sharp bones.

Small boys and girls enjoyed swinging. Swings were fashioned from thick vines that grew up the trunks and the branches of sturdy trees. Naya Nuki remembered a swing that went out over a deep pool of water. It was so much fun to swing out over the water and let go, plunging into the pool from high above.

Boys used poles to vault across streams or over fallen trees. Girls tried their skill with the poles, too. Naya Nuki had suffered a badly sprained ankle once when she had vaulted across a stream and landed on loose rock on the opposite shore. All cuts and injuries were serious. The only medicines available were herbs and their value was limited.

Some games were for boys only. War games were boys' favorites. Sticks were used to sling mud balls during mock battles. Those hit would fall as dead warriors do during a real battle. In other make-believe battles, the boys ran, jumped, and kicked each other. Knocking an opponent down meant he was "dead." The boys would play these rough games until they were exhausted. Girls were never allowed to play war games.

Boys also loved to wrestle. Two opponents would meet and try to throw each other over backward. If a boy could put his opponent on his back twice, that boy was declared the winner. Often bets were taken on who would win. Gambling made the contest even more exciting.

The day passed quickly, followed by another night and day. Naya Nuki's moccasins were wearing thin. Her feet were toughened to the rough walking. Her body was thin and hardened. Her face was dark and windburned. She had traveled hard for eleven days and was getting closer to her goal with each step. She walked through thick deep grass, over loose rock, among trees and bushes, and through shallow streams.

On her twelfth day, Naya Nuki felt more sure than ever that she would find her people, but her food supply was almost gone. She would need to find food soon. This might take precious time and slow her down.

Game animals could now be seen in every direction. Great herds of buffalo grazed on the lush prairie grass. They would scarcely move as Naya Nuki came close. Many times she had to circle around great herds of the giant beasts. She had no way of killing one of them and could only imagine how good a piece of the liver or the heart would taste.

There were more trees than ever now, giving Naya

Nuki many good places to hide in case of danger and providing her with many safe places to camp for the night. Even though she felt much safer now, Naya Nuki still remained alert to any sound, odor, or sight that might signal danger.

For several days Naya Nuki had carried a stick. She had sharpened one end of it with her knife. The wood was very hard. She could use the stick to dig roots, and as protection against snakes and wild animals. Wolves traveled the prairie in packs of ten or twelve and could be dangerous to humans when they were starving. Naya Nuki hoped she would never need to use her stick against attacking wolves, but she would be ready.

9 *Inches from Death*

The twelfth day was near its end as Naya Nuki looked for a safe place to spend the night. She found a large meadow that was almost completely surrounded by trees and bushes. Some of the bushes were chokecherry. Most of the berries had dried right on the branches but were still good to eat. Camas roots and wild carrots grew everywhere in this meadow. This would be a perfect place to spend the night, as it provided plenty of food and an excellent place to camp.

Naya Nuki felt happy at finding this wonderful spot. She laid her things down and began digging camas roots. She worked quickly and in just a few minutes had a nice pile of roots. She moved to another group of plants and had just started to dig with her stick when she was startled by a sound from behind her. In an instant Naya Nuki was on her feet and in a life-and-death run for the trees.

A mighty grizzly bear was coming up behind her as she was digging roots and was surprised when Naya Nuki suddenly jumped up and started running. The startled grizzly stood on its hind legs and growled loudly for a few seconds. This gave Naya Nuki a head start for the trees.

The great white bear dropped to all fours and ran

after her. The bear could run much faster in a straight line than Naya Nuki could, but she could change directions in an instant and dodge away from the charging bear. One blow from a powerful paw of this eight-foot, seven-hundred-pound giant and Naya Nuki's journey would be over forever. The great bear was gaining on Naya Nuki. She could hear it breathing.

With a final burst of speed, Naya Nuki reached the trees. She dashed between two trees that were so close together that the grizzly could not follow. While the bear went around the trees, Naya Nuki came back the same way and began a frantic climb up a tree. Without worrying about her arms and legs, Naya Nuki climbed like a cat. She tore skin from her arms and legs as some of the smaller dead branches gave way under her weight. The rough bark and pointed ends of broken branches scraped her bare skin raw.

The tree was not large, but Naya Nuki was able to get above the bear's reach just as the beast arrived at the base of her tree. The grizzly pawed at the tree with rage. Naya Nuki hung on as the tree shook violently. Just below her stood the most ferocious animal known to Naya Nuki and her people. Now Naya Nuki faced this great danger alone.

She had come just inches from death. The only thing that saved Naya Nuki was that grizzlies cannot climb trees. Unlike the smaller black bear, which has curved claws, the grizzly's claws are almost straight and useless for climbing trees.

Naya Nuki's buffalo skin and all her belongings except her precious knife lay on the ground a distance away.

The knife at her side would be useless against the powerful bear. Her only chance was to stay in the tree.

For ten minutes the angry bear shook the tree while Naya Nuki hung on tightly. Her arms and legs were bleeding, but she felt no pain in the face of such great danger. When the angry grizzly stopped shaking the tree, it prowled around and around the tree, roaring loudly. How long would the beast stay? The sun was setting and a cold wind began to blow. The grizzly showed no signs of leaving.

Naya Nuki's arms and legs began to ache. The small branches of this young pine tree would not support all her weight unless she put some of her weight on her feet and some on her hands and arms. For relief for her aching arms, Naya Nuki wrapped her sore legs around the thin tree trunk to take the load from her arms and give them a rest.

When her legs seemed ready to let loose, Naya Nuki gripped the tree trunk tightly with her hands, wrapping her arms around the trunk, so she could let her weary legs hang free for a few minutes of precious rest.

Naya Nuki clung to the tree, shifting her position now and then for some relief for her aching body. As darkness came, she could no longer see the great bear. The sky was cloudy, making the night pitch dark. The cold wind blew harder and harder. Naya Nuki did not dare come down. The bear could be waiting for her in the darkness below.

Naya Nuki was beginning one of the longest nights of her life. She was cold and sore. Every muscle in her body ached. The cuts, scratches, and scrapes on her legs and arms burned with pain. It seemed impossible to find a comfortable position in this small tree, but it was saving her life.

Naya Nuki never thought she could remain in the tree all night when the pain was so great. She changed positions often, trying to keep warm and find relief from the great soreness that gripped every inch of her body. Hour after hour she kept her determination to stay in the tree, safe from the claws of the great white bear.

The wind continued all night, and the air became colder and colder. Naya Nuki was suffering unbelievable pain when the eastern sky began to lighten. She strained her tired eyes for a glimpse of the ground beneath her. She must be sure the bear had left before she came down from her miserable perch. The sky was heavy with clouds and daylight came with painful slowness.

Finally Naya Nuki could see all around and was sure the great bear had left. Slowly she began to lower her aching body downward. Inch by inch she neared the ground. When her feet finally touched, she still clung to the tree to keep from falling to her knees. Her weary, aching legs quivered under her weight. Naya Nuki sagged against the tree, moving first one leg and then the other, trying to get her circulation back to normal. Circulation began to return slowly, but great pain racked her entire body. It was almost an hour before Naya Nuki could stand without holding to the tree.

In agony, Naya Nuki took her first steps on quivering legs. She moved slowly toward her abandoned buffalo skin and pile of roots. They all remained just as she had left them in her headlong dash for the trees.

Naya Nuki carefully lowered herself to the ground,

trying to move in a way that kept the pain from getting worse. She ached all over. It was hard to kneel. Once on the ground, she rolled her roots and other meager belongings into the buffalo hide. Then she got on one knee with her foot on the ground. Slowly she rose to her feet and painfully walked west once again.

It was very cold. The wind howled, and snow mixed with rain began to pelt Naya Nuki as she bent forward in her slow, stumbling walk. She had not slept all night. She headed for an outcropping of rock where she could crouch down out of the cold wind and miserable snow and rain. Here she unrolled her buffalo hide and crouched beneath it for warmth. She enjoyed some camas roots and soon in great weariness she dozed off to sleep.

Naya Nuki awoke in the middle of the afternoon, her body stiff and sore all over. Slowly she rose to her feet. Moving was very painful, but she was determined to continue. She walked on, still tired and very sore.

The longer Naya Nuki walked the better she felt. She passed carefully by an old Indian camp on her way west. This camp consisted of two large lodges made from timbers. The frames of timbers were only five feet high and were arranged teepee fashion in a circle. The timbers were covered with sticks, driftwood, and dry grass. The camp hadn't been used for a long time, and the lodges were in poor condition.

The wind had died down and only a light rain fell as darkness approached. Naya Nuki climbed a hill to some large rocks and found an overhanging rock to shelter her from the rain. As she sat looking out over the rolling prairie, the sun broke through an opening in the clouds and turned the prairie to a brilliant gold. She could see the great river winding its way from the west. Everything was still as the gold turned to orange and then purple. Soon all was gray again as the clouds covered the sun once more.

Huddled in her buffalo hide, Naya Nuki slept soundly. When she did awake, it was only to look, listen, and smell. When she was satisfied that there was no danger, she went back to sleep.

On her fourteenth day since her escape, Naya Nuki was still stiff and sore from her night in the pine tree, but she got off to a good start before the sun was up.

10

Food and Hides

The day was clear and very cold. The grass was covered with a white frost. The sun was just rising above the eastern horizon at Naya Nuki's back when she heard a commotion from the direction in which she was traveling.

Naya Nuki quickly hid behind some rocks and looked ahead to where a river flowed from the north. A herd of antelope, followed by a pack of wolves, bounded toward the river. Except for the river the wolves would never have caught the swift antelope. Antelope are not good swimmers, and Naya Nuki watched as the pack killed two of them as they struggled to cross the river.

Naya Nuki had gotten no meat since her escape. All the dried meat she had carried with her from the beginning was gone. She had eaten the last of it several days before. She craved the taste of fresh meat and began to think about the snares her people made to catch rabbits and squirrels for food. Naya Nuki had helped to make snares before but had never made one by herself. She would stop early this day and take time to make a snare. She could almost taste the meat she planned to catch.

After crossing a large but shallow river, Naya Nuki walked north along its bank. She soon found a good place to make a quick shelter from tree branches and pine boughs. Already the afternoon was clear and chilly. It would be a cold night.

With a shelter and a bed of pine boughs made, Naya Nuki set to work making a snare. She used thin strands of buffalo hide and green willow twigs. She remembered the loose knot that would slip and tighten around the leg or the body of any small animal that tripped the bent willow branch that would set off the snare.

Naya Nuki worked carefully. When she finished, she tried the snare by tripping it with a stick. It worked well the first time. With a few minor adjustments, it worked even better. She was proud of her work and wished her mother could see her fine snare. Now if only she could be successful and find an animal in her trap the next morning.

Naya Nuki found a game trail leading to the river and carefully set her snare. Her keen eyes and knowledge told her that this trail was used often by small animals on their way to a drink of clear, cool water. The game trail and her snare were a long distance from her shelter. A light breeze blew from the snare toward Naya Nuki's camp. Her odor would not be detected by approaching animals. She would sleep and check her snare at daylight.

Naya Nuki woke often during the night to listen, but the howl of coyotes and a steady breeze hid any sound that might come from her snare. She slept uneasily. As soon as it was light enough, Naya Nuki found a sturdy piece of wood to use as a club and carefully approached the snare. Her heart pounded with excitement as she neared the site. She moved without making a sound.

Her first view of the snare took her breath away. The

snare had been tripped, and she saw a movement. It was a big jackrabbit caught by its right hind leg. The large rabbit was exhausted from the struggle to free itself. Naya Nuki moved quickly. One blow to the head with the club and death was instantaneous. The rabbit hung limp in the snare. Naya Nuki felt weak and dizzy from her wild excitement.

Soon she had her knife out and began cleaning the rabbit. She removed the heart and the liver and ate them immediately. She did not dare to start a fire and would eat the whole rabbit raw over the days ahead. The meat was warm and tasted delicious. The heart and liver were small, and Naya Nuki ate a hip and a hind leg also. This part was tough and hard to chew, but no meat ever tasted better.

Naya Nuki stretched the hide over a frame that she made to fit it. She would carry this on her back as she traveled and let it dry. As Naya Nuki worked, she thought about the snare, how she made it by herself, and how it worked just as she planned. She was feeling confident. Yes, she would make it back to her people. Nothing could stop her.

With the leftover meat packed and the frame fastened to her back, Naya Nuki turned west again. She saw many deer, buffalo, and antelope every day. There were always wolf packs trailing along. They were constantly hunting, watching for the weak, the very old, the very young, and the sick. Any weakness was noticed right away by the keen-eyed wolves. Whenever an animal was weak enough, the wolves moved in swiftly, surrounding the helpless animal. Naya Nuki saw many kills during her journey. She would remain strong and alert, ready for any emergency. She would not end up as meat for the scavengers.

There were more trees now than before, but still the open plains stretched as far as Naya Nuki could see. She longed for the first sight of the mountains. The trees grew mainly near the streams, in ravines, and on the north slopes of the rolling hills. They made good places to hide.

Naya Nuki traveled uneventfully for two days. She found berries and roots, and ate small amounts of her rabbit meat at each meal. She ate only twice a day, in the morning and at the end of the day's journey.

On her eighteenth day Naya Nuki came upon a slow-moving porcupine, which she killed with a heavy piece of wood that lay nearby. It was an easy way to get some meat. The porcupine was large and clumsy and not difficult to kill. Naya Nuki rolled the animal over on its back and with her sharp knife opened the stomach cavity and removed all the inner parts. She took the heart and the liver and finished skinning the animal. She would not bother with this hide. She cut the meat in strips and laid them over a large rock. She worked quickly until only the bones and the hide remained. She gathered up the fresh meat and continued on her long trek.

Every night seemed colder than the one before. November was only two days away. Naya Nuki made fur-lined booties out of her jackrabbit hide. She turned the skin outward and with strips of hide she sewed the booties to fit snugly to her feet. Each night the fur would feel so good against her cold and tired feet!

Naya Nuki had almost worn through all her elk and deerskin moccasins. Soon she would have to use some of her precious buffalo hide to make more moccasins. She would wait as long as possible before cutting away any of her buffalo hide. She needed every inch of it to cover her at night against the bitter cold.

Naya Nuki always tried to stay in sight of the great river. It would lead her to the mountains and home. Without it she would be lost. It seemed like a great silent friend, always there, always leading her on to freedom.

Naya Nuki was careful to keep her distance from the river because of the many trails that followed the river or led down to it. She wanted to avoid the danger of meeting enemies on these trails.

Sometimes the river was hard to see and even completely out of view because of the rolling hills. On the nineteenth day the weather was sunny and warm after a clear, cold night. The warmth felt good to Naya Nuki as she moved west.

It was the middle of the warm afternoon when Naya Nuki first noticed a strange smell in the air. The odor got stronger and stronger. It was the smell of death, the smell of rotting flesh.

Naya Nuki came over a rise and stood at the edge of a clump of trees. She was surprised at how close she had come to the great river, which had turned to flow due north for several miles. She could look down at the water in the river not one-fourth of a mile from her. Now the smell of death was so strong that Naya Nuki could hardly stand to take a breath.

She looked up and down the river. On the opposite side was a steep cliff, more than one hundred feet high. At the base of this cliff, at the river's edge, lay a mass of dark forms. As Naya Nuki looked closer, she could hardly believe what her eyes were seeing. There lay the bodies of at least two hundred buffalo that had begun to decay.

Naya Nuki stood for several minutes, amazed at the scene of mass death before her. As she looked, she remembered the stories told about the prairie Indians who hunt buffalo in this unusual way. The animals had been chased over a cliff.

First one of the fastest runners from the hunting party is picked to disguise himself in a buffalo robe with a buffalo-head mask. This hunter moves out in the open grass to hide between the buffalo herd and the cliff above the river. The rest of the hunting party surrounds the herd on three sides. These hunters remain out of sight and move as close to the herd as possible. At a given signal, they all jump to their feet and begin shouting as they run toward the herd. Instantly the buffalo panic and turn in a stampede away from the hunters. A few lead animals set the pace and direction.

The disguised hunter waits until the stampeding herd is very close to him before he jumps up to begin his dash toward the cliff. Buffalo have poor eyesight. They think the disguised hunter is a real buffalo. The Indian must keep just ahead of the wildly charging animals. This way he becomes the leader. He runs to the very edge of the cliff and stops suddenly to dive into a crevice in the cliff. As the first of the herd reach the cliff, they try desperately to stop and turn away, but it's too late. They are forced over the edge by the frightened animals behind them. Before the herd can turn away, hundreds fall to their deaths on the rocks on the riverbank far below.

Sometimes the Indian disguised as a buffalo is killed under the hooves of the stampeding animals before he reaches the safety of the crevice, or is driven over the edge of the cliff with the helpless buffalo.

After the stampede, the hunters follow a safe route to the river's edge to take all the meat and the hides they need. The rest is left for the wolves, coyotes, ravens, and other scavengers. Much of the meat rots, giving off a horrible odor that can be smelled miles away.

Naya Nuki cautiously approached the pile of rotting bodies, scaring away some ravens and coyotes feeding there. She pinched her nostrils shut and breathed through her mouth to avoid the smell.

As Naya Nuki got closer, she noticed that the buffalo lying in the water had well-preserved hides. The cool water had prevented rapid decay. With her knife she skinned an animal that was almost completely under water. She worked quickly, taking only enough of the hide to make moccasins to replace her worn-out ones.

Naya Nuki did not feel safe in the open at the river's edge. She took the hide and hurried into the willows nearby, moving upwind from the smell. Here she scraped the hide and cut it into pieces, each large enough to make one moccasin. She stretched the six pieces of hide onto frames she had fashioned from willow branches. These six pieces of buffalo hide would make three pairs of fine moccasins, which should last for the rest of Naya Nuki's journey. Now she would not have to cut into her large buffalo hide that she needed so much on the cold nights in the open.

Naya Nuki was excited about her good luck at finding the buffalo kill. With each passing day she became more sure of making it home safely. Her good luck would soon change, however.

11
The End?

Naya Nuki moved away from the river that afternoon and took shelter for the night among some dwarf cedar trees that hid her very well. During that night Naya Nuki woke up as usual to listen and smell for any sign of danger. As she got up on one elbow, she began to shake. Her head swam with dizziness. Her stomach turned over and over. She burned with a fever and shivered with chills at the same time. Naya Nuki felt very weak and slumped back down under her buffalo hide for warmth. Her head pounded with pain. She was very sick and completely helpless.

The long night seemed endless and when daylight finally came, Naya Nuki felt even worse. It took all her strength just to sit up. When she did sit up her stomach seemed to come up into her throat. Soon she was vomiting until her stomach ached. When the vomiting ended, there was a sour taste in Naya Nuki's mouth, but she felt better for a few minutes. Then the weakness returned. Chills shook her body. She slumped back into her buffalo-hide bed.

What would Naya Nuki do? Just when she felt sure she would make it home, this terrible illness took all her strength and made her helpless. The night had been cold and damp. Clouds filled the sky, and the day was as cold and damp as the night had been. It threatened to rain.

Naya Nuki just lay in misery, not even caring about the weather, food, water, or safety. Her awful sickness made her forget everything. How long would she lie here helpless? What could she do to help herself? She felt so lonely. She longed for her mother, who always had been there when she was hurt or sick. Naya Nuki buried her head in her buffalo hide.

The day wore on. Afternoon came. A light rain drizzled down. In the cold and dampness Naya Nuki rolled and tossed. She burned with a high fever. Her throat was sore and her head pounded. She slept for short periods of time. Night came and with it even colder weather and then snow. The dwarf cedars helped shelter Naya Nuki from the wet snow.

All night Naya Nuki suffered. It was a long, long night and it seemed day would never come. When daylight finally came, the snow changed to freezing rain, increasing Naya Nuki's misery.

For the second day, Naya Nuki did not move from her buffalo hide. She felt no better. Sitting up made her feel worse. She began to wonder if this would be the end of her trip, the end of her daring try for freedom, even the end of her short life. She felt so sick she almost didn't care if she lived or died.

Another miserable night followed, and Naya Nuki's twenty-second day began clear and sunny. The warmth brought new hope to this sick and weak Indian girl.

Naya Nuki raised up on one elbow to look around her. Her lips and tongue were dry, sore, and cracked. Water from the melting snow dripped from the small

cedar trees above her. Naya Nuki cupped her hands to catch some water. She drank it slowly from her trembling hands. The water soothed her parched throat. Immediately she began coughing. Her stomach ached as the water reached it. Naya Nuki slumped back under her buffalo hide. She would rest for a while and then try to move. She knew she must do something to help herself, or she would die in this lonely place.

When Naya Nuki did sit up again, she felt weak and dizzy. Her legs were wobbly as she stood up, clinging to a small tree. The sun was warm and the snow was melting fast. Still she shivered and shook all over. It was all she could do to pick up her belongings and stumble toward a distant grove of large pine trees.

Naya Nuki had to stop often to lean against a tree for rest. The grove of trees was on the edge of a low ridge. The other side of the ridge sloped down to a river valley, which was a mile wide.

Naya Nuki reached the ridge and sat down to rest her weak and aching body. Her head rested against a tree. Her eyes were closed. It was then that a strange smell reached her sensitive nostrils. No, it wasn't a strange smell. She remembered it from somewhere in her past but could not remember exactly where or when she had smelled it before.

Naya Nuki sat for some time, resting and trying to remember where she had smelled this odor before. Then suddenly she remembered. It was a smell she had known as a small child. Her people knew of places in the mountains where hot water poured from the earth. Naya Nuki had visited several of these places as a small girl. The hot water had a strong smell. Her people bathed in the hot water and gave it to those who were sick. They drank it as a cure for many illnesses.

Naya Nuki moved slowly in the direction of the odor. In a meadow of thick green grass she found the spring. Water was oozing toward the river. It was hot, and the sulfur smell was very strong.

Naya Nuki lay flat on her stomach, lowered her head, and drank the hot, bitter-tasting water. The short walk had exhausted her. After drinking the hot sulfur water, she found a hiding place in the willows nearby. The day was warm, and she was soon sound asleep.

When Naya Nuki awoke, she felt much better, though still weak and wobbly on her feet. She returned to the spring for another drink. Then she was sound asleep in her hiding place once again.

The next time Naya Nuki woke up it was dark and much cooler. For the first time since her illness, she felt hungry. She ate a little from her supply of porcupine meat, berries, and camas roots. Again she drank from the hot spring. The bitter-tasting sulfur water was helping to fight the illness that made her feel so miserable and helpless.

Naya Nuki lay awake for a while listening to the sounds of the night. Then she fell asleep again. The sun was well up before Naya Nuki awoke. She had slept for almost twenty-four hours since her first drink from the hot spring. She still felt weak and shaky, but her strength was returning.

Naya Nuki moved slowly into the open area on the hillside to get a better view of the valley below. Once again she was thinking about the danger of being recaptured and danger from wild animals.

Naya Nuki could see a great distance into the valley as it stretched out before her, running from north to south toward the great river. The land had not changed much since she had left the place where the Yellowstone River flowed into the great river, but ahead she saw more hills, more trees, and many more rock formations carved out by wind and water. Naya Nuki remembered this river valley and knew she was more than halfway along in her struggle to get back to her people.

She was still weak. Her moccasins were worn through, and there were many miles of rough travel ahead. Each day there seemed to be a greater hint of winter in the air. Naya Nuki decided to rest one more day. She remembered that she had left the six pieces of buffalo hide on their drying frames under the dwarf willows where she had become so sick. She must go back for the pieces of hide. She would spend the day making three new pairs of moccasins.

The snow had all melted. Naya Nuki went in search of the six pieces of buffalo hide. In the daylight she could see dwarf cedars in every direction, but the right spot could not be far away. It took her an hour to find the right clump of cedars. She picked up the frames and returned to the willows near the hot spring.

The pieces of hide were not as dry as they should be, but Naya Nuki could not wait. She quickly went to work on the first moccasin. Her knife had become almost like a friend to her. She used it every day of her journey and constantly checked to see if it was still tied to her side. Its loss would be a serious loss indeed.

Naya Nuki worked smoothly, cutting the hide to the

proper size and shape to fit her foot. She cut strips of hide to use as thread. She cut holes along the edges of the hide so the strips could be passed through easily.

Naya Nuki worked most of the day, stopping only to drink more of the hot sulfur water and to eat from her food supply. Her strength was returning steadily.

When the last moccasin was finished, Naya Nuki looked at the three pairs of beautiful new moccasins. She threw away her old ones and pulled on a new pair. She walked to a lookout spot and her new moccasins felt so good on her feet. Once again Naya Nuki was eager to be moving and again excited about reaching freedom in the mountains, but she needed another night of rest first.

Back at the hot spring Naya Nuki remembered how her people dammed up the hot water, making pools for bathing. She would do the same now.

First she gathered rocks and used them to make a small circle around the spring. With her knife she loosened clumps of sod to pack between and behind the rocks. As she worked the water began to fill the circle. The small dam grew in height until the water was two feet deep.

Naya Nuki removed her elkskin dress and her new moccasins and lowered herself slowly into the warm water. Naya Nuki felt so relaxed, so warm. She moved to the side of the pool and lay back, resting her head on a clump of sod. She rubbed the warm water over her face. She rolled onto her stomach and put her head under water. Getting up on her knees, she ran her fingers through her hair to remove dirt and dust that was caked there. She rubbed her legs and arms, washing away dirt and dead skin left from scratches and cuts she received climbing the tree to escape the grizzly bear.

When she was finished cleaning her body and hair, Naya Nuki once more lay back to enjoy the relaxing feeling the hot water brought to her small, weary body. She lay still for thirty minutes. Her eyelids became heavy, and she almost fell asleep. When she lifted herself from the wonderful hot pool, her skin was wrinkled from being in the water so long. She felt better than she had since beginning her lone run to freedom. That night Naya Nuki slept soundly.

12
Moving West Again

At first light Naya Nuki got up. She headed straight for the hot spring, first for one more drink of the bitter-tasting water and then for another bath.

After eating some berries, roots, and porcupine meat, Naya Nuki began her twenty-fourth day of travel west. Her illness had cost her four precious days. Now she was eager to make up for it.

It took Naya Nuki only one hour to reach the river in the valley below, and since it was November the water was very low. She was able to wade all the way across.

After crossing the river, Naya Nuki made her way through the willow flats and up the next ridge. She walked among the pine trees. As she reached the top of the rise, Naya Nuki stopped suddenly, stunned by what she saw. A dozen braves on horseback were coming right at her from only one hundred yards away.

Had they seen her? Naya Nuki stood frozen in her tracks, unable to move. The slowly-moving riders were not looking her way. She had not been seen yet. Where could she hide? She did not dare move for fear of being seen. Slowly she looked around her. To the right was a growth of shrubs. She would hide there. Then she saw the horse trail just on the other side of the shrubs.

That was where the riders would pass. She would be found if she hid there.

Naya Nuki lowered herself slowly until she was lying flat on the ground. Cautiously she crawled to the left, crossing a fallen tree and lying as close to it as possible. It barely hid her from view, but it must do. It was her only chance.

The sound of the horses grew louder. Naya Nuki could hardly breathe. Her hands trembled. What could she do if the riders should see her? She would run through the trees. She would climb rocks. She would do anything to get away. She would run like the wind.

The riders were not talking to each other. The first one was now only twenty-five feet away, passing the shrubs and moving over the ridge and into the trees. They were headed into the river valley that Naya Nuki had just left.

She lay very still. It seemed to take the riders so long to pass by her. Then the sounds became fainter. Naya Nuki lifted her head very slowly for a look. One glance and she lowered her head quickly and held her breath. One of the riders had stopped. He was checking the load that he had tied to the back of a second horse. He hadn't seen her, but Naya Nuki was not out of danger yet.

When Naya Nuki took another look, the rider still had his back to her. She saw a dog that had been trailing along behind the last rider. Suddenly the dog picked up Naya Nuki's scent and started coming toward her. It would be sure to give her away!

Naya Nuki reached for her knife. When the dog got to her, she would kill it with her knife and then run for

her life, hoping the hunters would not follow her because they were leading pack horses. She would cut the dog's throat with one stab and then run.

Naya Nuki clenched the knife in her right hand. The dog was only twenty feet away when suddenly a pair of jackrabbits jumped from cover directly in front of the charging dog. The two rabbits bounded off to the left, with the startled dog in pursuit. At the same time the last rider mounted his horse and continued on the trail, paying no attention to the dog or the rabbits.

When the dog and the rider were both out of sight, Naya Nuki rose to her feet and ran away in a bent position. She ran for five minutes before she came to a small stream. Naya Nuki walked into the ankle-deep water and stayed in the water, walking up stream in a northerly direction. This guaranteed that the dog would lose her scent and would not be able to follow her.

The bottom of the stream was rocky, which made travel slow, but Naya Nuki walked as fast as possible for more than a half-mile before she left the stream and ran west. She stayed out of view as much as she could, keeping in the trees and the willow bushes wherever possible.

Several hours passed before Naya Nuki felt reasonably safe again. She stopped in some bushes on a high hill and looked all around for signs of danger.

The land was rougher now, more rocky and with higher hills. There was a small mountain on the horizon ahead. Naya Nuki recognized it from her journey east with her captors. Remembering the landmarks was helping her. She knew she was getting close to the real mountains. As she continued to look ahead, she saw another small peak just north of the larger one. Today the small northern peak is called Bear Paw Mountain, and the larger southern one is named Highwood Peak.

Naya Nuki knew that she was nearing the giant waterfalls of the great river. Soon she would be on familiar ground. Yet she knew she was still a long way from the mountain shaped like the beaver's head that marked the way to the valley of her people.

Naya Nuki was excited as she looked out at these two peaks. She was also very tired from her run. Her recent illness had taken its toll on her strength. She would have to stop for the night sooner than usual.

As she rested on the hilltop, Naya Nuki noticed ravens circling and landing about a mile away and below her. As she looked more closely, she saw a small column of smoke rising near the circling ravens.

Carefully Naya Nuki walked over the rocky hills toward the site. She stayed low and hidden among the rocks and the trees. Soon she could see what was attracting the ravens. The ravens, along with six coyotes, were feeding on the carcasses of two buffalo. Naya Nuki knew this must be the place where the hunters she just passed had made their kill. They had built a fire to cook some of the meat before moving east.

The wind began to blow and dark clouds were moving in from the southwest as the day neared its end. Naya Nuki moved closer to the kill. The ravens and coyotes saw her and moved away. After making sure it was safe, Naya Nuki walked over to the dead buffalo. The hunters had taken only the hide and the hindquarters for meat. The front halves of the animals were left to the scavengers. The meat looked delicious and was there for the taking. Naya Nuki worked quickly, slicing away long strips of meat. She put these with her food supply and then wrapped other strips of meat around a thick green willow branch.

The fire still contained a deep layer of hot coals. Naya Nuki chewed some chunks of raw meat while she roasted other strips of meat on the willow stick. Soon she propped the stick over the hot coals to let the meat roast until it was golden brown. She quickly cut more willows and wrapped strips of meat around them. Now there were six branches holding roasting meat over the coals.

Naya Nuki had cut the meat very thin to make it cook quickly. She was at the site for only thirty minutes. All the time she was there she watched nervously for danger. Darkness was coming rapidly. She quickly picked up the sticks and moved off into the fading light.

The wind blew stronger now, and the temperature was dropping. Naya Nuki headed for an outcropping of rock that was surrounded by low-lying shrubs and stunted trees. She found a huge boulder that had fallen against an even larger one. She crawled into the space under the leaning boulder and soon cleared a level spot large enough to stretch out in and sleep.

The leaning boulder gave her a front door and a back door. Naya Nuki piled rocks up, making a three-foot wall at both ends of her cozy shelter. The roasted meat was delicious. Naya Nuki ate her fill and put the rest of the meat with her other food. She slept soundly, waking up only twice during the night. The wind howled, but the rock walls protected Naya Nuki as she slept. Finding the buffalo meat was a wonderful piece of good fortune.

At the break of dawn, Naya Nuki was on her way once more. The wind was very strong, the sky cloudy, and the temperature below freezing. The mountain that marked the closeness of the giant waterfalls of the great river seemed to get further away instead of closer. Clouds hid the top of the peak as Naya Nuki crossed several rivers and hiked in and out of three different valleys. Her legs and feet carried her over rocks, through sagebrush and grass, and never failed her.

When Naya Nuki stopped for the night, the smaller peak to the north was very close. Her last look from the hilltop showed the great river winding southward from the west side of the small mountain. She remembered this turn and knew she was about two days from the giant waterfalls. There were herds of buffalo in every direction. She found shelter from the wind in a dense clump of pine and cottonwood trees.

Her twenty-sixth day started with a breakfast of cold but cooked meat and dried berries. The wind was bitter cold and blowing hard. The sun came out of the clouds in the early morning and the sky cleared, but the wind blew even more.

Naya Nuki walked with her head down. Her eyes were burning from the blowing sand and dust. She found relief where the trees were dense enough to break the wind.

Naya Nuki's feet were hardened and tough, but prickly pear grew everywhere and was hard to avoid. Her feet were sore and swollen. She soaked them in each stream she had to cross. The cold water felt good on her aching feet. She picked berries, as she did nearly every day. Even the shriveled berries tasted good.

13 *Mountains!*

As she liked to do at the end of each day, Naya Nuki climbed to the top of a hill. She looked west and on the horizon she saw what looked like great white clouds. A closer look and Naya Nuki knew she was looking at the shining mountains of her homeland. She danced around a big rock with great joy and excitement. She was going to make it after all! Nothing would stop her now! Naya Nuki was the happiest girl in the world. She danced and danced with joy.

Naya Nuki was up early the next morning, still excited about seeing the high mountains. It was late afternoon when Naya Nuki heard the distant roar of falling water. She was approaching the giant falls. She was about seven or eight miles from the falls when she found shelter in a ravine for the night.

Again Naya Nuki was on her way at first light. The wind was just a gentle breeze. The sound of the waterfalls was much louder now. Spray rose from the falls in the distance like a column of smoke.

From a hillside Naya Nuki got her first glimpse of one of the waterfalls. She saw a flat sheet of water, two hundred yards wide, dropping about eighty feet to the rocks below. The beauty was breathtaking. This was only one of the giant waterfalls. There were others spread along the great river for miles. Each waterfall had its own beauty. In several places there were islands in the middle of the river between the falls. Spray from the falling water caught the sun's rays, creating a beautiful rainbow over the foaming river.

For her whole day of walking, the great river came from the south. The land was familiar. Naya Nuki did not need to worry about becoming lost, nor did she need to wonder about how much further she had to go. She knew she was not many sleeps from the place where the great river was formed by three separate streams. Near the three forks of the great river was the place of her capture on that awful day more than three months ago.

From the three forks it would not be far to the valley of her people. Naya Nuki left the falls and walked southwest over a nearly treeless plain. There were so many buffalo that she had to go out of her way to avoid the beasts.

The snow-covered mountains loomed nearer than ever as Naya Nuki found a tree-filled gully to spend the night in, safely hidden. The gully was on a hillside where she had a good view of the valley in both directions. Naya Nuki liked a campsite with fir and spruce trees. In minutes she could have a mattress of boughs. Rolled up in her buffalo hide, she slept comfortably.

Naya Nuki was up even earlier than usual, more excited than ever to be on her way. She was still careful not to move too fast over ridges and hills. She didn't want to come as close to riders as she had done before. She ate several strips of buffalo meat and some berries as she walked slowly along in the predawn darkness.

She was saving the cooked meat until last. It would not spoil as fast as the raw meat would.

The morning was clear but very windy and cold. By afternoon dark gray clouds moved in from the west. A sudden hailstorm forced Naya Nuki to take cover in a dense growth of spruce trees.

The hailstorm lasted only ten minutes but dumped almost an inch of hail on the ground. The wind blew steadily as Naya Nuki was on her way again. The day continued cloudy and windy with some light snow. Naya Nuki was making good time. Low mountains were now very close on the south side of the great river. Today these are called the Big Belt Mountains.

Naya Nuki stopped at dark after hiking steadily. Each night she was tired, but always was careful to take time to pick a well-hidden campsite for the night. She never stopped to eat during the day. She ate from her food supply while on the move. Each evening she enjoyed eating slowly after finding a safe campsite. She would eat only enough to keep up her energy. She made sure she would not run out of food. Often she would stop just before dark to dig roots or to pick berries to add to her supply. She always kept a reserve supply of food. No matter how hungry she was, she never wanted to eat the last bit of precious food.

Naya Nuki spent the night at a place where the great river flows from the south and even a little southwest. The banks of the river were rocky and more than twenty feet high in places. The river was more crooked here than it had been for some time.

Naya Nuki resumed her journey before daylight on this, her thirtieth day. She came closer to the great river than usual and came upon an Indian road that caused her to run to its edge with great excitement. It wasn't a real road, just a well-worn horse trail about eight feet wide in places and full of ruts. Naya Nuki had been on this road several times with her people and had walked this way as a prisoner a few months before.

Excitedly Naya Nuki examined the trail. The tracks were old, but in places she could easily see that the last hoofprints left were made by horses headed south. Could these be the tracks left by the horses of her people as they were returning from their annual buffalo hunt? Naya Nuki felt like running down the road. She was so excited that it was hard to think, but she calmed down. She knew better than to stay on this road. It could be very dangerous. Unfriendly Indians could be using it, and she might be discovered.

Naya Nuki turned and left the road to follow it at a safe distance. She angled away from the road and moved toward some willow bushes. The willows were not unusual, but something else had caught Naya Nuki's attention. What she saw now was even more exciting than finding the road. She ran to the willows for a closer look. Then she was sure of it. Here were at least twenty small shelters formed from willow branches. She herself had made many shelters exactly like the ones she was standing next to now. Naya Nuki's mother had taught her how to construct such a shelter, and Naya Nuki and Sacajawea had slept in one the night before their capture.

Naya Nuki ran to several other willow shelters as if to make sure they were real, and that she was actually standing next to them. These shelters were made by

Shoshonis, her people. Her excitement was so great that she felt like calling out to her people right where she stood. Instead she left the shelters, walking as fast as she could. Naya Nuki was headed home!

There was very little game now. There were no buffalo and very few elk or deer. Naya Nuki did see some antelope and a few mountain sheep on the high ridges. When she was near the river or a stream coming down out of the mountains, she saw many beaver and some otter. There were lots of serviceberry bushes and some currants.

When darkness came, Naya Nuki hated to stop. The great excitement of this day made her want to keep going. Naya Nuki would start even earlier the next morning. She climbed a ridge and found cover in some shrubs.

The next morning, Naya Nuki walked on the hillside above the road and followed close to it as it climbed over a low mountain pass. This route cut off many miles that would have been traveled by following the winding river. After she crossed the pass, Naya Nuki found that the river valley widened. She kept in sight of the road and the rivers.

Soon Naya Nuki saw another familiar sight. The great river ahead was coming out of two walls of steep rock hundreds of feet high. Lewis and Clark would come by this exact spot in four years and call these spectacular rock walls the Gates of the Mountains.

The deep gorge carved by the mighty river is more than four miles long. Naya Nuki passed the gorge and came to a large valley where the river spread out into wide channels with islands here and there. She recognized this valley and knew the three forks of the river were close now. She crossed a creek she remembered visiting before with her people. They had come to this creek to find minerals used in making white paint. Naya Nuki had stood at this exact spot several times during her lifetime.

With every step Naya Nuki's excitement grew. Her legs were strong and her lungs and heart were tuned to her vigorous days of hiking from dawn to dark. Naya Nuki was very thin but in good health. She drank large quantities of water, as her body used great amounts of liquids. Her dark brown eyes were always on the lookout for danger. It was very difficult for Naya Nuki to get to sleep after so much excitement at seeing such familiar sights. This night she rolled and tossed and finally dropped off in a restless sleep. The November night was very cold and clear, but there was no wind.

Before dawn Naya Nuki was up and eating. Her food supply was getting low, but she did not want to take the time to gather berries or dig roots. She was eager to keep moving every minute that it was daylight. She knew she was getting close to home and her excitement gave her added energy and determination.

On this morning, her thirty-second day, Naya Nuki stopped to look at the Indian road and the great river below her. She saw deer and antelope on a distant hillside. There were geese and ducks in the quiet waters of the river. She saw a beaver working on a dam on a small channel of the river. A pair of otters swam nearby. It was a scene of peaceful beauty. There were still many islands in the river, and the water was clear now. The bottom of the river was covered with colorful rounded rocks. Naya Nuki did not show much interest in the scenery. This was the day she would reach the three forks and would soon stand at the exact spot of her capture more than three months before.

Naya Nuki walked faster than ever, but her way was slowed by the many creeks she had to cross on her way. Most of these streams were dammed up by the work of many beavers.

Finally Naya Nuki made her way down closer to the road to avoid the deep beaver ponds. She saw many signs of horses that had traveled the road. There were tracks and droppings. None of them looked very fresh. She took a detour back up the long ridge when she saw a grizzly sow with two cubs just ahead of her. A bear with cubs is more dangerous than any other bear. Naya Nuki went far out of her way to keep the huge bear from seeing her.

It was just getting dark when Naya Nuki reached the three forks on the great river. She had hoped to be further than this, but it seemed that the more excited she became the longer it took to do everything.

Naya Nuki looked at the great river as it was formed by three smaller rivers. She followed the one nearest to her that flowed from the southwest, from her homeland.

Before it was completely dark, Naya Nuki found a place to camp. She walked a short distance up a creek and made a bed in the dense willow bushes. She gathered some berries, wild carrots, and roots in the near-darkness. She ate one strip of buffalo meat, a few roots, and some berries. A drink of clear, cold water completed her meal, and she rolled up in her buffalo hide for some much-needed rest. Sleep came very slowly, and Naya Nuki was restless and woke up often. She was eager for morning to come, eager to be on her way, to reach her people, to be safe at last.

Again Naya Nuki was up and ready to start well before daylight. She could sleep no longer. At first light she moved away from her campsite in the willows. About four miles from the three forks, she stopped and looked at a special spot on the river. Many memories flashed through her mind. This was where Sacajawea and Naya Nuki were taken prisoner on that awful day.

Minutes later Naya Nuki turned and moved away at a quick pace. She knew how close she was. She might see her people any day now. Carefully she approached the Indian road to look for signs. Again she saw hoofprints and dung, but still no fresh signs. There was a damp chill in the air. The higher mountains were covered with dark clouds, and the wind was blowing harder every minute. But Naya Nuki was not noticing the weather. Her eyes were busy taking in the familiar sights all around her.

14 *Stopped*

Naya Nuki continued on her journey, looking for fresh signs. She found another camp, the spruce frameworks of more huts still standing, but she could tell it was not a fresh camp. The weather worsened as the day wore on. Snow began to fall. Naya Nuki stopped. She sensed that this was not just a brief snowshower.

Quickly she turned back to the spruce frames and hurried to make a storm-proof hut. Her hands were skilled at weaving new branches very tightly through the framework of an old hut. She left the needles on branches to seal most of the cracks so the hut would shed the snow and rain. Around the sides of the hut she wove tight walls, and put several extra layers of branches on the top of the hut, making them hang down over the sides for added protection.

Naya Nuki worked in a blinding snowstorm and soon the ground was covered with a white blanket. After the repairs were completed, a very cold Naya Nuki went to work digging roots and gathering dried berries from nearby serviceberry bushes. The snow was ankle-deep when she crawled inside her snug little hut with her supply of roots and berries and her other belongings. There was still plenty of daylight left, but the storm made travel impossible and dangerous. Mountain storms could last for days and dump two or three feet of snow in just one day. The high winds could whip up drifts more than ten feet deep.

The storm raged all afternoon and into the night. Naya Nuki was cozy and warm in her spruce hut. She came out once in a while for a look. Her hut was covered with snow, but inside it was still dry and much warmer than outside. Naya Nuki lay in her buffalo hide enjoying her berries and roots. She even slept off and on. The night seemed long and still. The snow-covered hut cut out all outside sounds, as the storm continued all night long.

Naya Nuki did not know when daylight came. She was asleep in the darkness of her hut. Her doorway was blocked with a deep drift of snow. When she did wake up, she dug her way out and was amazed to see so much snow. It was still snowing heavily. The snow was more than knee-deep and some drifts were shoulder-high.

Naya Nuki returned to her hut, realizing she was trapped and could not move from her shelter without risking her life. Would this be the end of her journey? Would this have to be her home for the winter, alone without help? Would she die here so close to home and safety? What should she do? Naya Nuki knew any decision could mean her life or her death.

Naya Nuki sat in her hut, measuring her supply of roots and berries. How long could she last? Could she get more food, enough to survive? She carefully divided her food into small piles, each one representing one day's supply. Each pile was a tiny amount, just enough to keep her alive from day to day. Naya Nuki counted

the piles. There were only eight, but somehow she would manage. No, nothing would stop her from reaching her people. She had been through too much to fail now!

Naya Nuki spent her time inside her hut, coming out often to see if the snow was still coming down. It seemed that the storm would never end. Night came, then another day and another night as the storm raged on. Naya Nuki was patient. She would not leave the shelter of her hut until she was sure it was possible to move on safely.

After three long days the storm finally had passed. The snow was forty-two inches deep on the level and the drifts were seven or eight feet high in places. Naya Nuki made a path around her buried hut. She had felt like a prisoner during the storm.

It was still impossible to move very far. Naya Nuki looked about. At a distance of a half a mile stood a clump of tall cottonwood trees. After careful thought she decided to make a path to the trees. The trees would give her a good chance to climb above the snowdrifts for a better view of her surroundings. Something had to be done to find a way out of this white prison.

Naya Nuki began the long struggle to reach the trees. The deep snow was wet and heavy. She stamped it down as she moved forward. It was exhausting work. She stopped often to rest and catch her breath. In some places the snow was over her head and very hard to pack down. Naya Nuki was getting wet and cold. Several times she went back to her hut to get warm, but she did not give up. She would not give up. She must make it to the trees. Somehow she knew the climb to the top of one of those trees would help her escape this prison of deep snow.

It took Naya Nuki most of the day to reach the trees, which were further than she had thought at first. She was so tired that she knew she would have to wait until morning to make the climb safely. It was getting dark. The light would be better in the morning. Wearily, Naya Nuki walked through her long ditch in the snow back to her hut. Her main worry now was the wind. If the wind blew hard during the night, her path could be completely filled by morning and all her work would have to be done again. She lay down in her hut to eat and sleep, hoping the wind would not blow while she slept.

Each time Naya Nuki woke up during the night she listened. Each time she heard no wind. The night was calm. Morning came with the day bright and clear. It was very cold. It took a while for Naya Nuki's eyes to adjust to the brightness of the sun on the pure white snow.

In the bitter cold Naya Nuki walked to the cottonwood trees. She picked one of the tallest trees that was also the easiest to climb and started up the lower branches. Taking care not to fall, Naya Nuki reached the top safely. She had a good view of the entire valley and could see for miles. She quickly looked around, studying the area for any signs of life, and then began a slower, more careful survey of the valley and the mountainsides surrounding it.

On her second search of the valley, Naya Nuki's eyes caught sight of a long dark shadow on the distant snow. It looked like a track, much like the path she had made to this tree. The direction was southeast. It was impossible to tell what kind of tracks these were or even the direction of travel of whatever had made the tracks. At least there were tracks. There was a sign of life. This gave Naya Nuki hope.

Naya Nuki sat on a branch, her eyes glued to her exciting discovery. She began thinking. These could be the tracks of elk or deer moving to the winter range in the lower valleys. They could be the tracks of enemy warriors. And they just could be the tracks of her people. Naya Nuki was so excited that she felt like moving toward the tracks immediately, but she had learned from experience that it is better to wait, to think things through, then choose the best plan and follow it carefully. She did not want to make a mistake now. She was so close to her goal.

Naya Nuki decided to stay in the tree and watch the tracks patiently. She had the urge to start toward the tracks immediately, but decided to wait and watch instead.

The sun warmed the cold air as the morning wore on. Naya Nuki studied the distance between her tree and the tracks. In a direct line the snow was very deep, but off to her left she saw a slight ridge curve toward the tracks. She knew the snow would not be as deep on the crest of this small ridge and, even though the distance would be further, the snow there would be much easier to travel through. That would be her route when she did leave for the tracks.

Naya Nuki decided to stay in the tree until the sun was directly overhead. Then she would begin to make her way toward the tracks. They might give her a chance to escape this snowbound valley. She would head for the tracks whether she saw anything or not. Naya Nuki did not take her eyes off those tracks in the distance.

By the middle of the morning, Naya Nuki was weary of sitting in her high perch. Suddenly her eye caught a movement and she raised herself to her feet on the high branches for a better look. Something was moving along the track. She watched anxiously, her heart pounding in her chest. It was a horse and rider, then another, and another. Naya Nuki strained to see anything that would tell her whether the riders were friends or enemies, but it was impossible to tell from that distance. She watched as more than twenty riders moved slowly south along the snowy track.

Naya Nuki's excitement increased when she saw others walking behind the riders. Some of those who were walking were leading horses, and some were women and children. These could be her own people heading to their winter home from the buffalo hunt, but it was late in the year to be returning from the hunt. They could be members of a warring tribe, but they would not have women and children with them. No, this was a peaceful tribe. Women and children never traveled with war parties. Naya Nuki would follow them and get close enough to find out.

She quickly climbed down from the tree, gathered up her belongings, and started the difficult struggle to reach the tracks. The tracks were three or four miles away. Naya Nuki worked her way slowly through the deep snow to the low ridge she had seen from her perch high in the cottonwood tree. It took her a long time to reach the ridge. At the base of the ridge the snow had drifted so deep that it was over her head. It was almost dark when she reached the crest of the ridge, where the snow was only a foot to eighteen inches deep.

Naya Nuki did not stop when darkness came. The sky was clear, and a bright moon shone down, lighting the snow-covered land. Naya Nuki followed the crest of the ridge and made better time. The snow did not build up on the crest as it did on the flat ground. Still the travel was slow and tiring. In some places the ridge dipped down, and the snow was much deeper. Naya Nuki was traveling only half a mile each hour but was making steady progress toward the trail made by the riders. The night wore on. The moon worked its way across the sky. Now Naya Nuki was struggling hard to keep going. She forced her weary legs to take each step. Often she had to stop, gasping for breath and waiting for renewed energy to go on.

When the moon went down, the darkness forced Naya Nuki to stop. Soon she was digging into a snowdrift for shelter and a place to rest while she waited for daylight to come. Her snow cave was a welcome relief from her exhausting day and night of travel through the snow. Naya Nuki was too tired to sleep. She rubbed her sore legs, ate some roots and berries, and stretched out in her buffalo hide to rest. Her rabbit-fur moccasins felt good on her cold, wet feet. She dozed a little but did not really sleep.

15 *A Day to Remember*

When dawn came, Naya Nuki slowly crawled from her snow cave and lifted herself to her feet. Her muscles were stiff and a little sore, but after more than one thousand miles of travel, Naya Nuki could take almost anything and snap back quickly. Her tough leg muscles loosened soon and once again she was struggling through the snow toward the tracks. She knew the way to go by looking toward the mountains that she had sighted from the treetop the day before.

She hadn't traveled far when suddenly she broke through the snow and onto the horse trail. She looked in both directions and then turned right and headed south, the same direction she saw the riders going.

Now the walking was easier. The horses had cleared a wide trail through the drifts. The track was still snow-covered and harder to walk on than bare ground. Naya Nuki moved as quickly as possible over the rough trail.

By late afternoon Naya Nuki came to another camp. There were many snow caves and other places where the snow had been cleared and fires built. The horses had packed a large area of snow near the camp while they searched for something to eat beneath the white covering. The way the camp had been set up made Naya Nuki quite sure that these were Shoshonis, some of her people. She didn't stay long but moved on faster than ever.

Naya Nuki knew she was about six hours behind these travelers. She walked on as fast as she could. It would be dark before she would catch up, but the moon would make travel at night possible. One thing she worried about was a breeze that started blowing just before sundown. A little snow was blowing into the trenchlike trail. If the wind blew harder, travel would become more difficult.

Naya Nuki continued on into the night. The wind picked up, and the blowing snow began to accumulate on the trail. She was slowing down, but her excitement kept her going. Conditions got worse and still she pressed onward. Her rest stops became more frequent and lasted longer. Finally she had to stop to wait for the first light of day. She huddled in her buffalo hide against the side of the trail and out of the wind.

Naya Nuki was tired from lack of sleep and her long struggle to catch up with the travelers. She was warm in her buffalo hide and dozed off to sleep sitting up.

When she awoke, Naya Nuki saw that daylight was just coming to the eastern sky. The wind had stopped blowing, but there was more than a foot of blown snow in the track. Naya Nuki quickly ate a few dried berries as she hurried along the track. She hoped to catch up with the travelers before they broke camp and moved further away.

The tracks led over a low ridge and down into another open valley. The full light of day had just arrived. Naya Nuki looked down the sloping ridge, and she saw the camp below her. The band was packing and preparing

to leave. They were about a half a mile from where Naya Nuki stood.

She paused for a few minutes to look at this fascinating sight. Yes! These were Shoshoni Indians. They were dressed like Naya Nuki's people. I have found my people, thought Naya Nuki. I have come home! I am safe! With a burst of speed Naya Nuki's feet carried her at top speed down the snowy path. She hardly felt her feet touch the ground. Naya Nuki was so excited, so happy, she ran faster than ever. All her tiredness was forgotten. A surge of energy filled her thin body.

When she was halfway down the slope, suddenly a brave on horseback moved his horse into Naya Nuki's path from behind a huge snow-covered boulder. Naya Nuki tried to stop but slipped on the snow and slid underneath the horse. The frightened horse nearly stepped on her.

The rider jumped down and grabbed Naya Nuki, pulling her to her feet. The young warrior and Naya Nuki could hardly believe their own eyes.

"Cameahwait!" shouted Naya Nuki.

"You! It cannot be. You have returned. How? Where? What?" asked Cameahwait. He could not believe this could be Naya Nuki. His eyes must be lying. But no! This was she.

Both danced around, embracing, looking at each other again and again. Tears streamed down Naya Nuki's face. She had succeeded. She had survived. She had escaped. She was home to her mountains, to her people. She could not believe it was real. It all seemed so strange, much like a dream instead of real life.

Cameahwait scooped Naya Nuki up in his arms,

mounted his horse, and rode off to the camp, shouting the good news as he rode. The rest of the tribe had just started leaving the campsite when they heard all the noise. They saw Cameahwait riding swiftly toward them, holding Naya Nuki in front of him. They all turned to watch this strange scene.

Cameahwait pulled his horse to a stop and jumped down, still holding Naya Nuki. No one could believe it was really Naya Nuki. Some thought the spirits were playing tricks on their eyes. All moved closer for a better look. From the back of the crowd came Naya Nuki's mother. She knew it was no trick. This was her little Naya Nuki. She had come back! She was alive!

Naya Nuki ran to her mother and threw her arms around her mother's neck. The tears flowed freely as mother and daughter cried for joy. It was a scene that no Indian standing there would ever forget. It was a story that would be told around Indian campfires for years to come.

It was a long time before things quieted down enough for Naya Nuki to answer questions. Then the questions came. "Where is Sacajawea? Where are the others who were taken prisoner? How did you escape? How long and how far have you traveled?"

Naya Nuki answered the questions the best she could. Then the chiefs ordered all to leave. They had to get out of the high mountain valleys before more bad weather came. They must return to their winter valley.

Naya Nuki saw many horses loaded with buffalo meat and hides. The hunt had been good. The tribe had gone later in the year to avoid another attack. They had done very well and were now hurrying to their winter quarters.

Naya Nuki learned that one of her brothers had been killed in the battle and that her father was still recovering from a bad wound. Naya Nuki's head was bowed and the news brought tears of sorrow to her eyes.

Naya Nuki was fed and allowed to ride double on Cameahwait's horse. Cameahwait asked Naya Nuki many questions about his sister, Sacajawea. He hoped she was well and happy.

Several days later the tribe reached the winter camp in the Lemhi Valley. There was no snow at this lower elevation. A great campfire was held just to hear Naya Nuki tell her amazing story. After a feast on buffalo meat, Naya Nuki began her story. She was afraid to speak at first, but then the story began to come easily and she spoke far into the night. Not a sound was made as all the tribe listened to this fascinating story. It was all so unbelievable. Each person listened in amazement. No such story could be made up by a young girl such as Naya Nuki. Yes, it was true. They were hearing one of the greatest stories of their lives. Naya Nuki's story would be repeated by many Indians around campfires for years to come as this girl and her journey to freedom would become a legend.

When Naya Nuki finished her story that night, the chiefs held council and announced to all present that this girl-child's name would be changed. From now on she would be called Naya Nuki, which in Shoshoni means "Girl Who Ran." You see, we don't know Naya Nuki's name before this courageous journey took place. We do know that Indian names were changed when great deeds of courage were done. Probably no eleven-year-old girl has ever shown more courage or greater love for her people than did Naya Nuki, the Girl Who Ran.

Epilogue

It was four years later in the month of August that the *tabbabone* came. Lewis and Clark were looking for the Shoshonis. They needed horses to continue their expedition to the Pacific Ocean. There was great excitement among the tribe at the arrival of these strange-looking men with pale skin and with hair on their faces.

The greatest day of all was August 17, 1805, when a second group of the Lewis and Clark Expedition arrived at the Indian camp. As Captain Lewis wrote,

> We drew near to the camp and just as we approached it, a woman made her way through the crowd toward Sacajawea, and recognizing each other, they embraced with most tender affection. The meeting of these two young women had in it something peculiarly touching, not only in the ardent manner in which their feelings were expressed, but from the interest of their situation. They had been companions in childhood. In the war with the Minnetares they had both been taken prisoner in the same battle. They had shared and softened the rigours of their captivity until one of them escaped from the Minnetares with scarce hope of ever seeing her friend relieved from the hands of her enemies.[1]

1. Meriwether Lewis, *The Lewis and Clark Expedition*, Archibald Hanna and William H. Goetzmann, eds., three volumes (Philadelphia and New York; J. B. Lippincott, 1961), vol. 2, p. 334.

Naya Nuki and Sacajawea had much to talk about. Naya Nuki learned of Sacajawea's life and marriage to the French guide, Charbonneau, who was hired by Lewis and Clark for their history-making journey to the Pacific Ocean. Naya Nuki begged to hold Sacajawea's tiny son. So it was that Sacajawea and Naya Nuki met again on this happy and historic day.